W9-BGZ-542

BIKERS PLAY FOR KEEPS

Charley Benjamin leaned forward in his chair and put both palms flat on Dennison's desk. "Your typical mafioso doesn't want any attention. He's happy to stick to extortion, loan-sharking, pimping, quiet stuff, so he can live in a big house in a nice neighborhood next door to doctors and lawyers and politicians and pretend he's just another upstanding citizen.

"The biker doesn't give a shit for any of that. His universe is the outlaw life, and anyone not part of it is an enemy—and the biker is absolutely ruthless toward an enemy. It's total retaliation. If a man mouths off, stomp him; if a woman mouths off, rape her. If someone—anyone—looks like a real threat, kill them.

"They play for keeps and they're too mobile, too strong, and too ruthless to stop with conventional methods. It's like trying to fight guerrilla terrorists in their home jungles, using traditional military strategy. Long before the law-enforcement folks realize this, the bikers are going to take over."

"Don't be too hard on the regular cops," Miss Paradise said. "Sometimes the cops don't like it either, but they've got to play by the rules."

Benjamin smiled. "But you don't."

"Why should we?" Dennison snapped. "The bikers sure as hell don't."

Dennison's Warriors were ready to rev up their engines.

HELL
ON
WHEELS

Adam Lassiter

BANTAM BOOKS
TORONTO • NEW YORK • LONDON • SYDNEY • AUCKLAND

DENNISON'S WAR: HELL ON WHEELS
A Bantam Book / June 1985

ISBN 0-553-24951-7

Published simultaneously in the United States and Canada

Bantam Books are published by Bantam Books, Inc. Its trade-
mark, consisting of the words ''Bantam Books'' and the por-
trayal of a rooster, is Registered in U.S. Patent and Trademark
Office and in other countries. Marca Registrada. Bantam
Books, Inc., 666 Fifth Avenue, New York, New York 10103.

PRINTED IN THE UNITED STATES OF AMERICA

H   0 9 8 7 6 5 4 3 2 1

For Dorrit

Qui desiderat pacem, praeparet bellum.
[Let he who desires peace prepare for war.]

—VEGETIUS
De Rei Militari

Exterminate all the brutes.

—JOSEPH CONRAD
Heart of Darkness

The Mexico-Arizona Border, West of Nogales
The 4th of July

The saguaro cactus looked eerily like a sentry. It was as tall as a four-story building, a thick fluted column reaching into the night, with two symmetrically curved arms, raised as if in benediction, or warning. Beyond the saguaro the desert rolled off to the west, windswept dirt and rock outcroppings dotted with clumps of creosote bush and prickly pear. There was no moon, but the sky was cloudless and thick with stars, and the barren landscape was bathed in their pale greenish glow.

Chicken Charley the Child Molester looked up at the saguaro and frowned. Something about this run put him on edge—but then, he'd been edgy most of the time lately. He'd been riding with the Satan's Sons for years and he'd been on a dozen of these border putts, two already this summer. He knew how to handle himself, and besides, what kind of fool would mess with a pack of righteous Sons in the middle of the goddamned desert? Still, he heard that warning bell way off in the back of his mind, dinging faintly. . . .

Either that, or he'd been going a little too heavy on the reds and Gallo. Chicken Charley smiled grimly into the darkness.

They'd hung the Chicken Charley nickname on him along with his colors. It wasn't a wisecrack about his courage;

1

it referred to his big Adam's apple. He won the rest of his handle after he'd been riding with the bros for maybe six months. It was in a miners' saloon over in Bisbee, and Charley made sure the bartender knew where he'd disappeared to; he wanted the bros to find him in that back room. It was the first chance he had to show real class in front of them. When he and the chick came back out, they whooped and called him every kind of badass name they knew. Someone poured a beer over his head, and the chick pulled up her T-shirt and showed them her tits. The next morning they added the rest of his tag, and Chicken Charley the Child Molester knew he was in, a full-on bro for sure. The chick claimed she was eighteen, but Charley figured she was fourteen, tops.

He realized he was grinning, and quickly wiped the expression off. The whole club was making this run—eighteen sullen men in leather and denim, sitting on their silent Harleys and squinting into the darkness—and no one was real happy about it. Although it was two in the morning, the temperature was still hovering around ninety degrees, and the air was dry as parchment. Besides, this was the holiday, and they'd been planning the run up to the rodeo in Prescott for a month. Hell, you'd always party hearty at that blowout. You could live for the whole weekend on the Indian fry bread they sold in the plaza, the cold brew from the joints along Whiskey Row, and all the strange ginch you and your dick could stand.

"Fucking greasers," someone muttered into the darkness. There were murmurs of agreement. None of the Sons liked Mexicans—not even Pancho Rauncho, even though the little brown bastard was Mex himself. The goddamn beaners were like dogs: you'd kick 'em, and they'd come back to lick your freakin' hand. The other clubs in the Outsiders network got dope, or whores, or porno—and the Sons got the fucking beaners, on the fucking Fourth of July. Still, the Mex were easy money, and all the clubs had to pull their load.

The pack of bikes faced a ravine that marked the border, a kind of dry concrete-lined moat about twenty feet deep with sides sloping at better than forty-five degrees. Along the center line of the bottom was an eight-foot chain-link fence topped with three strands of barbed wire, but here, at the point marked by the solitary saguaro, a four-foot section, wide enough for a bike to pass, had been cut out, the wire bent back.

"Smoke 'em if you got 'em, bro." The guy parked next to Chicken Charley passed him a joint. Charley hesitated, then took a shallow hit, not inhaling. The sweet smell of marijuana drifted on the night air, and Charley could see the winking tips of other joints being passed among the silenced bikes. He gave the roach back to the other guy. The alarm bell in the back of his mind was tapping out a message: here was a fine night *not* to get fucked up.

"Yeah," the guy next to him said. His name was Scuz; he wore a droopy walrus mustache and was always chewing on the ends. It was probably the way he got his nourishment, Charley figured; the 'stache was always stiff and matted with the remnants of Scuz's last meal. "What we need is a little shot of booster-cable, yeah, bro," Scuz went on, as if Charley had spoken. He took a plastic vial from the pocket of his greasy denim cutoff, thumbed off the cap, and shook two little white pills into Charley's palm.

"Roses are shit, violets are rank," Scuz recited. "Whenever I'm down, I hit on the crank." He leaned over and plucked a half-full can of Coors from the next biker's hand, popped a couple of the methamphetamine tablets into his mouth, and drank.

What the hell, Chicken Charley decided. Maybe the crank would rev his motor. At least he knew the speed was righteous; their brother club over near L.A., the Disciples, made it themselves in their own lab. He took the proffered can and washed the two tabs down with a couple of swallows of the warm, half-flat beer.

3

"Hey, Rodge," someone called in a low voice. "Those fucking beaners ain't gonna show, is what I think."

Rodger the Dodger sat on his Harley at the head of the pack, staring out over the ravine. The Satan's Sons club president was a massive three hundred pounds troweled onto a 6-6 frame, topped with a wild mane of ratty shoulder-length red hair and matching beard. Unlike most of them, he was in the habit of considering a matter before exploding into mindless viciousness. That's why he was president: the bros respected a thinker. They also respected the fact that when Rodger the Dodger did blow up, he went absolutely insane. They all knew about the time Rodger stopped for a six-pack in an Indian bar outside Santa Fe a couple of years back. The way Charley heard it, it took four ambulances to cart off the Indians that tried to hit on Rodger. Rodger walked out of the joint on his own two feet—with the six-pack.

"Easy, bro," Rodger the Dodger called over his shoulder. "We are going back loaded with paying beaners, or someone is gonna get his greaser ass kicked."

Before anyone could argue, a flashlight flared from across the ravine, flicked off, then shone twice more in a quick semaphore.

"Aw right," Rodger announced. "Let's do it."

Charley stood on his starter and kicked it down, and the big Harley 74 engine caught immediately. All around him the night exploded with the unholy roar of dormant bikes bursting back to life. Bros who had been drowsing in their saddles a moment before were now sitting up straight and bright-eyed, twisting accelerators, smiling grim smiles of satisfaction as Milwaukee iron revved and tailpipes spit backfire.

Rodger the Dodger raised his left hand in a fist, brought it down, and plunged his bike over the lip of the ravine.

The rest of the Sons followed without hesitation, forming into a single file as if they had been assigned places. They had not—but every one of them was a superb motorcyclist. Few of them were athletic, or had even played sports in high school; most had hefty guts that testified to a daily ration of several six-packs of beer. Yet on his bike, every man had the raw grace and agility of a mounted hussar; the combination of man and machine was more potent than either of its component parts, radiating power and domination and suppressed rage.

Chicken Charley shot over the lip of the ravine and down the near wall in barely controlled freefall, a cycle length from the man in front of him. He hit bottom, dropped into low gear, and met the far wall in a hill-climbing throaty scream of horsepower, shooting up toward the stars as if launched. He came up over the edge, got air for a moment, bounced down on his rear tire, and slewed around in a dust-raising stop.

The Mexicans looked to be all there, eighteen of them: men, women, a couple of adolescent boys, looking frightened and hopeful at the same time. Near the front of the group was a woman—a girl, actually, maybe seventeen, darkly beautiful in American jeans and a blousy scoop-necked top that showed the upper swell of full breasts. She didn't look scared at all; she was smiling at the group of bikers like a kid flirting at a school dance. Charley knew the others were eyeballing her too, and he thought, *Shit. As if they didn't have enough to worry about already.*

"*Bueno,*" Rodger the Dodger called out to the group. "Pick yourself out a bike, each of you—and have the money ready. *Dinero.*" He rubbed thumb and forefinger together. "Five hundred, in dollars—and don't no one try nothing funny. Then be ready to ride. We ain't got all night, and we are going to fly—so you'd better be ready to hang on, because anyone falls off, we ain't going back to pick up the pieces."

"I got me a piece I'm gonna pick up." A biker named Footlong pointed a finger at the girl in the low-cut blouse. He was a tall scrawny dude, who was called Footlong because that's what he claimed to be toting between his legs. "Over here, *señorita*," Footlong called to the girl. He pronounced the Spanish like an obscenity.

The girl turned her smile on him. She glided to his bike, swinging her hips provocatively.

Chicken Charley drew a little guy who was maybe fifty; about half of his teeth were gone, and the ones that were left were black. His breath smelled like rotten meat. Charley riffled through the wad of bills the old man handed him— mostly crumpled tens and twenties—then stuffed the money down inside one of his black leather boots. "Hang on, Pops," he said over his shoulder. At least the guy didn't weigh enough to slow him down.

The crack of a hand across flesh cut the air, and the girl with Footlong gasped. Footlong backhanded her again. "Bitch don't have the money," Footlong called to Rodger.

"Dump her."

Footlong clamped a hand over one of the girl's big breasts and squeezed hard enough to bring tears to her eyes. "Aw, what the hell, Rodger," he said, staring at the girl. "She'll pay—we'll figure something out." He showed the girl a slavering leer. "Won't we, *señorita*?"

Chicken Charley the Child Molester felt a vague jolt of nausea in the pit of his gut. But what the hell, the woofie knew what she was letting herself in for.

The bikes shot back through the ravine—Charley heard the Mex gulp as they dove down toward the hard concrete floor—and then they were racing across the open desert, the bikes paired up in run formation, Rodger the Dodger and Footlong at the head of the pack. Charley started to relax. There was something in the speed of the run, the bike throbbing between his knees and the warm air whipping at his long hair, that always calmed him.

The green INS four-wheel-drive carry-all spotted them before they'd gone three miles. The bullhorn PA speaker mounted next to the windshield squawked and then an authoritative voice boomed across the desert, but Charley couldn't

6

make out the words above the cycles' basso engine noise. Rodger the Dodger kicked his bike up to 100 mph, and simultaneously, as if they had received a telepathic order, the other bikes accelerated to match the pace. Charley shot a quick look over his shoulder, in time to see the Border Patrol wagon jounce over a rise, settle with a bone jarring jolt, and pull to a ragged stop. A 4WD cager was no match for a chopped scooter.

They cut Route 286 fifteen minutes later, stringing out along the two-lane blacktop and cutting back to a smooth 70 mph cruising speed. Within a half-hour they made the outskirts of the strip along 86, the lights of downtown Tucson shimmering to the east. They dropped the greasers in the back parking lot of a hamburger joint. A zit-faced high-school kid holding a dripping mop opened the back door and stared at them. "Hey, whaddaya think you're doing?"

Rodger the Dodger turned toward the kid and pointed a forefinger at his chest. The kid stumbled back inside like he was shot. The wetbacks milled around, muttering to each other in Spanish, wondering what happened now.

"Not you, mama—you're with Footlong."

The scrawny biker had a visc-lock grip on the pretty girl, who was half-dismounted from the rear seat of his scoot. She glanced around, appealing for someone to side with her. The other Mexicans looked carefully away.

The bikers stared at her hungrily.

"Mount up, mama," Footlong ordered. "We're gonna have ourselves a night."

The girl gave him a wan smile and climbed back on the scoot. The little dinging bell in Chicken Charley's head changed pitch.

The Satan's Sons clubhouse was in the rear of a scumhole bar the gang owned under the name of a shyster lawyer. All of the bros had arrest records, and most of them had convictions, so they couldn't hold a liquor license. The shyster charged them plenty, but it was worth it, because it gave the club control of a high-cash-flow business. The dough they took in from coyoting wetbacks went through the bar and came out clean as fresh linen.

The turn-out room was upstairs. There was a big four-door upright cooler against one wall, stocked with cold Coors, a bare red-tinted light bulb in a ceiling fixture, a swaybacked sofa with springs poking through the red-velvet upholstery, and a half-dozen mattresses strewn around the bare plank floor, all of them filthy and spotted with dried beer, urine, and semen. The Mexican girl looked around and managed a brave smile. The bros stood around her in a rough semicircle; Footlong held her by the wrist.

The girl licked her lips. "I am with Futlon'," she said. "Futlon', he is my boyfran'."

Someone laughed mirthlessly. Chicken Charley's gut spasmed. The two hits of crank he'd taken were kicking in, but the warm body-high was absent. All he felt was jaggy.

"I saw her first, bros." Footlong's hands began working the massive brass buckle on his razor-strop belt. "You can fight it out for sloppy seconds."

Chicken Charley could see that the girl still did not understand. She watched Footlong drop his denims, still smiling weakly. She owed him and she would pay. That was fair. It would not be too bad. It would be over quickly enough.

But that's not the way it went; Chicken Charley had been in on enough of these scenes. Footlong yanked open the front of the girl's jeans, skinned them roughly down over her hips. *"Por favor,"* the girl muttered.

"Yeah," Footlong grunted. *"Por favor,* mama."

The guy's ass was small as a pair of baseballs, and he didn't pump for more than twenty seconds before he went limp. Before he got his pants up again, Rodger the Dodger was between the girl's legs, forcing them apart, thrusting into her like he was knifing someone. The girl started to scream and Rodger punched her in the jaw. The scream degenerated into a groan.

Chicken Charley looked toward the door and thought about sneaking out. It was too risky. He had the idea that some of the bros had been looking at him suspiciously lately as it was. The crank was eating holes in his stomach, as if he had drunk a beaker of sulfuric acid.

Cloth ripped, and the girl's breasts swung free. One of the Sons dropped to his knees and began slobbering all over them. Rodger the Dodger pulled out and someone else took his place. Chicken Charley saw wetness glisten between the girl's thighs. Her dark eyes sparkled in the unnatural red light, flashing pain and panic.

By the time it was his turn the girl was moaning deliriously, her face feverish with sweat and terror. Her body stank of the ones who had gone before him, and as soon as he was inside her he went limp. Her eyes opened and looked into his from inches away, and for a moment she seemed aware again. But then she looked past him to the pantless guy waiting impatiently for his turn, and her pupils dilated and went dull.

Charley got off her, hitching at his jeans as he stumbled from the room. Behind him he heard the hiss as beer cans popped open, and the laughter of the other bros. He figured they were laughing at him and did not care. He barely made it out the back door to the parking lot before dropping to his knees and spewing beer and bile onto the pavement.

Dennison's Compound
The 9th of July

"There's something about a tall chick," the biker said. He let his eyes travel the length of Miss Paradise's body. It was a long trip; she was six feet tall barefoot, and her cowboy boots added another two inches. The biker's leer drifted back up until their eyes met.

"I look at a tall chick," the biker said, "and I get to thinking how much fun it'd be to leave a tongue trail from her toes to her tits, and back." The biker chortled, and the sound had as much to do with good humor as a sneer has to do with a smile.

Miss Paradise returned his gaze expressionlessly. She wore jeans, a western-cut checked shirt with nacre buttons, and a matching neckerchief. Her buttery blond hair was tied back in a bandanna, and her face was un-made-up, except for two spots of red on her high cheekbones that could have been natural color. Her eyes were dark blue, and the line of her perfect jaw and long neck were classical as Grecian sculpture.

The biker looked suddenly away, as if he had been caught at something he should have had more class than to attempt. Dennison cleared his throat. "My dear, meet Chicken Charley the Child Molester." He smiled politely.

"All right," Miss Paradise said neutrally. She perched half her butt on the edge of Dennison's desk. The biker was in his mid-thirties. His white T-shirt was streaked with gray dirt, his black denim pants stained with grease and motor oil; for a belt he wore a polished length of motorcycle drive chain. Over the T-shirt he wore an equally dirty blue denim jacket from which the sleeves had been raggedly cut. On the back was a round patch, about eight inches across: a laughing, horned devil's head, surrounded by licking red flames. Above the patch was stitched in red thread: "Satan's Sons MC" and below it, "1%er."

"Like the threads?" the biker asked. He tried to make it sound like some kind of challenge, but the bluster suddenly seemed forced.

"Who's your tailor?" Miss Paradise drawled. "Frederick's of San Bernardino?"

Dennison drew open the curtains of the double-wide

floor-to-ceiling windows that dominated one wall of his office. He was of medium height, somewhere in his forties, his dark hair flecked with a touch of gray here and there. People who met him for the first time usually got an impression of stoutness and languor, especially if he were seated behind his desk; in fact Dennison's thick body was hard and toned, and he moved with unlikely quickness and grace.

It was midmorning, but this far north the sun climbed quickly in summer, and light spilled into the comfortable room. Dennison unlatched one of the glass panels and eased it open.

"Fresh air," Miss Paradise muttered. "There's an idea." Dennison shot her a quick tight smile. She did not have his patience. She might reserve judgment on their scruffy visitor for the moment, but she expected answers, and quickly.

Dennison's desk was baroquely fashioned hardwood, with feet that curled into the thick rug and a work surface big as a bed. It was always covered with a mound of memos, magazines, open books lying spine-up, computer printouts, and letters, as if someone had upended a trash basket on it. When Miss Paradise found it necessary to look for some item in the pile, she often discovered forgotten artifacts: a half-cup of coffee topped with a skim of greenish congealed cream, a birthday card, his telephone. Yet Dennison could come up with whatever he needed almost instantly.

Four overstuffed armchairs upholstered in dark leather faced the desk in a semicircle. The biker sat in the one at the end away from Miss Paradise. Dennison settled down behind his desk.

"You'd better take it from the top, Charley," Dennison said.

"Good idea." The biker offered his hand and a sheepish grin to Miss Paradise. "The name is Charles Benjamin."

Miss Paradise looked at him narrowly. In the few minutes since she had entered the office, the man had undergone a subtle metamorphosis, as if his bloated arrogance had been pinpricked and his personality deflated. The filthy clothes, the stubble-face, the greasy long hair, were still there—but the provocative insolence in his look and manner and tone of voice was gone, leaving only a rather thin and ordinary man who needed cleaning up.

"Charley is an agent for the Department of Justice," Dennison said, as if that explained everything.

Miss Paradise was not particularly impressed. "What do you want?"

"Your help."

Miss Paradise pursed her lips. She took a pack of Marlboros from the pocket of her checked shirt and speared a cigarette between two long fingernails. She started to put the pack away, then offered it to Benjamin. Dennison nodded, as if that were the signal for the start of serious business.

"What do you know about the outlaw motorcycle gangs?" Benjamin asked.

Dennison shrugged noncommittally. He knew quite a bit—it was his business to track the shifts and balances among the scumbags of the world—but he'd learned long ago that you do not learn anything new listening to yourself.

Miss Paradise found Dennison's heavy brass desk lighter under a four-week-old copy of *The Wall Street Journal* and held flame to the tip of Benjamin's cigarette. "The original outlaw bikers were World War II vets who were out of work and out to raise some hell." Benjamin exhaled smoke. "The first most people heard of them was when about four thousand rode into Hollister, south of Frisco, on the Fourth of July weekend in 1947. They drag-raced on the main street, kicked in some windows, and got a big spread in *Life* magazine. The same thing happened every couple of years afterward, and each time they got coverage, because they were good copy. You take a photo of a three-hundred-pound bearded guy with an earring, wearing denim and sitting on a cycle, and a chick with big tits and no bra behind him, and you put it on the cover, you will sell magazines. All the same, even if the bikers were obnoxious and halfway vicious slobs, they weren't hard-core criminals."

Charley Benjamin took a deep drag on his cigarette. "That started to change in the late sixties. The bikers had always been drug users; drinking, doping, anything that put you out on edge, that was part of the life. It took them twenty years to figure it out, but finally they got the idea that there was big money in dealing. They already had the apparatus for narcotics trading: a tight-knit organization, contacts, mobility."

Dennison tapped his fingers on the arm of his chair. "Then there was the intimidation factor."

"Right," Benjamin agreed. "A smashed kneecap here, a razor slash there—a murder if necessary—and pretty soon there was no competition. By the mid-seventies the outlaw bikers controlled ninety percent of the meth in northern California, and were running the stuff all over the country. They set up labs and turned it out themselves. There's a lot of money in speed, and they used it to branch out. In 1979, two hundred agents of the DEA, the BATF, and other agencies pulled a simultaneous raid on southern California biker hangouts. They came up with a carload of automatic weapons, enough ammo for a small war, and a pound of pure crystal meth. They prosecuted under federal racketeering statutes, and at the trial the U.S. attorney claimed the bikers produced a hundred thousand dollars' worth of meth every day, and laundered the cash through Mafia connections and Swiss bank accounts. The more cash they took in, the more they branched out—prostitution, loan-sharking, protection rackets, the works."

"What did the authorities do about all this?" Miss Paradise asked.

"They sent me in."

"Okay."

Benjamin stared down at the carpet and shrugged. "I got the assignment because I'd been there before. After high school I rode with the Blackjacks. I liked the partying and the biking, but there were other things I didn't like so well. After about six months I quit."

Benjamin looked from Dennison to Miss Paradise. When neither of them reacted, he went on in a soft monotone. "I joined the Army. I was assigned to Special Services and went to Nam. I did two tours. While I was there, I ran into some guys who worked for the Agency; Nam was full of spooks back then." He stared pointedly at Dennison.

Dennison returned the gaze. Charley Benjamin's tone and mood changed with dizzying rapidity. Dennison recognized the symptoms of a man who had been pushed over some psychic cliff and was clawing and scrambling to get back on solid ground. Dennison's hunch was that Benjamin's operational days were over, at least until after he took a long period of R&R.

"I was recruited as soon as I got back Stateside," Benjamin said. "I worked part-time for the Agency while I went to college on the G.I. Bill, and when I graduated I became a special agent.

"At the time I was infiltrated, the antibiker operation was slated to become Priority One." There was a note of bitterness in Benjamin's tone. "We ran a full scenario: I 'quit' the Agency and they got me a job with an armored-car service. I embezzled ten thousand bucks from them, made sure they found out, and drew two years at Lompoc. At the time, half a dozen Satan's Sons and a couple of Blackjacks were doing time there on narco raps. I knew a couple of the Blackjacks from the old days, and they got me in with the Satan's Sons. I was paroled from Lompoc after seven months, and I was a probationary member of the Sons a week after that. A couple months later, I was initiated."

"In the meantime," Miss Paradise guessed, "the Agency was mounting a support operation?"

"In the meantime," Benjamin said, "the Agency was not doing shit. A couple months after I got out of the pen, there was a national election. The new President appointed a

14

new Agency head from his own political party. The new chief didn't have any patience for long-term deep-cover work. It cost too much, and besides, the public never heard about it, so there wasn't any publicity value for the administration. Officially, they told me to sit tight and proceed; unofficially, I was out in the cold.''

Benjamin leaned forward in his chair. "Let me tell you about the outlaw biker gangs. We are not talking fun-loving macho creeps. We are talking about a sophisticated nation-wide criminal organization. They sell dope, guns, and women. They own legitimate businesses in every major city—bars, massage parlors, porno shops, video arcades, anything with a high cash volume that allows them to launder money. They run motorcycle shops, freight companies, pawnshops, discount electronics outfits—for altering and marketing stolen goods.'' Benjamin leaned forward and stubbed out his cigarette in a heavy green-glass ashtray on Dennison's desk. "They are big, Dennison. They are goddamned big, and they have to be stopped.''

"Does this organization reach to the national level?'' Dennison asked.

"Just about,'' Benjamin said. "Over the years, the two strongest clubs worked out a territorial division: today the Outsiders control the West, the Mad Dogs have the East. Each gang runs a couple dozen satellite clubs—branch offices—and each satellite works a local territory. The Satan's Sons, the club I was with in Tucson, smuggles drugs and illegal aliens from Mexico. The Outsiders take fifty percent of the profits.''

"A franchise,'' Dennison murmured.

"Fifty percent is a hell of a cut,'' Miss Paradise said. "What does the local club get for the money?''

"A benefit package,'' Benjamin said wryly. "Like any corporation. The Outsiders supply protection, intel, and so on. They pay off cops, they provide extra muscle when it's needed. If a bro is arrested, his legal expenses are paid, and if he goes down, his family is taken care of until he's sprung. There's even a pension plan if he lives long enough to collect, and death benefits if he doesn't."

Dennison stared at Benjamin. "You took a big risk coming here."

"I had no choice. There's going to be some changes— and if they're allowed to take place, the bikers may be unstoppable, even by you, Dennison."

"What kind of changes?" Miss Paradise asked.

"The Mad Dogs—the big club in the East—has a new president, some guy who calls himself Apeman. Nobody knows much about him, but there are rumors he took over by stepping on a few bros who got in the way. About the same time Apeman started his takeover, the ranking officers in the Dogs started turning up in odd places. The New York City cops fished a couple out of the East River. Someone had removed their heads and legs with a chain saw. A couple others turned up in a garbage dump, welded inside fifty-five-gallon drums. You get the idea."

"How did the Outsiders react?"

"At first it didn't concern them—until a couple months back, when two Outsider satellites were ambushed during a run. A couple of bros were killed. The Outsiders got the message: Apeman plans to roll over them and take over the whole damned country."

"Then it's the Outsiders' move," Miss Paradise said.

Benjamin nodded. "The Outsider president is a guy named Rock. He's smart enough to realize that open warfare will hurt everyone. It draws attention and bad press, and it interrupts day-to-day activities, which stands to cost Rock and his clubs a lot of money. So I'm guessing Rock will try to set up some kind of alliance—and if he pulls that off, we are going to be looking at a criminal machine that will make the Mafia look like a social club."

Dennison leaned back in his chair and clasped his hands on his chest. Miss Paradise looked annoyed. "Why come to us?'' she asked Benjamin. ''Why don't you go to your own agency?''

''I did,'' Benjamin said angrily. ''I had to break cover to do it, which meant I was risking my life for them—again. The Justice people told me to sit tight, they'd take care of it. They'd appoint a panel to look into it right away. Shit,'' Benjamin added with heartfelt disgust.

''Let's face facts.'' Dennison's pleasant voice went hard. ''Conventional law-enforcement agencies don't have a chance against the outlaw bikers. While the feds are arguing with the state and local cops about jurisdiction, the bikers are staking out new territory like the Spanish conquistadores.''

Benjamin looked at Dennison with renewed interest. He nodded. ''That's not all. The bikers have their own people in place on the inside, so they're usually about three jumps ahead. A few of their contacts are cops on the take, but most are girlfriends they've worked into jobs with the police, state agencies, DMV, credit bureaus, telephone companies, the works. You put an undercover cop on the bikers' asses, and they know who he is the moment he hits the street. If he gets too nosy, he's dead—cop or no cop.''

''It's hard to believe,'' Miss Paradise said.

''You don't have to take my word. It's been documented in the press a half-dozen times in the last year or so. The bikers are too mobile, too strong, and too ruthless to stop with conventional methods. It's like trying to fight guerrilla terrorists in their home jungles, using traditional military strategy. Long before the law-enforcement folks realize this, the bikers are going to take over.''

''Don't be too hard on the regular cops,'' Miss Paradise said. ''Sometimes the cops don't like it either, but they've got to play by the rules.''

Benjamin smiled. ''But you don't.''

''Why should we?'' Dennison snapped. ''The bikers sure as hell don't.''

''The bikers play for keeps,'' Benjamin agreed. ''The

conventional law-enforcement agencies have been able to bring several cases against bikers, you know; they're not just lying down and letting those bastards walk over them. They spend a lot of time and money to get them into court—but when the case is called, there's always one item missing.''

"Witnesses," Dennison said.

"Yeah. They tend to get real forgetful before they get on the stand—or real dead.''

Charley Benjamin leaned forward in his chair and put both palms flat on Dennison's desk. "Your typical mafioso doesn't want any attention. He's happy to stick to extortion, loan-sharking, pimping, quiet stuff, so he can live in a big house in a nice neighborhood next door to doctors and lawyers and politicians and pretend he's just another upstanding citizen. The biker doesn't give a shit for any of that. His universe is the outlaw life, and anyone not part of it is an enemy—and the biker is absolutely ruthless toward an enemy. It's total retaliation. If a man mouths off, stomp him; if a woman mouths off, rape her. If someone—anyone—looks like a real threat, kill them.

"If you do get solid evidence on a biker, you've got to find him," Benjamin said. "It's almost impossible using by-the-book methods. They all go by nicknames, and most of the time your own bro doesn't know your citizen name. They don't have credit cards or checking accounts or known addresses. They can hit the road instantly, carrying everything they need on their bikes, and find a safe house in any of the dozens of cities where there are affiliate clubs.''

"They must have some kind of communication network," Dennison said.

Charley Benjamin dug a double-sized billfold from the back pocket of his jeans; a length of motorcycle drive chain secured it to the similar chain he wore as a belt. He pulled out a couple of dog-eared business cards and handed them to Miss Paradise. She glanced at both sides of the top one, then passed the cards to Dennison.

The first one read, "Ten-Ton Tony, Diamondbacks MC." The others were the same: a name, affiliation, and nothing else, in unadorned letters printed on embossed white card stock. On the back were as many as a dozen phone numbers, all but the bottom one crossed out.

"They've been developing the system for twenty years," Benjamin said. "The phone numbers always get you some bar or gas station or whorehouse. You say you want to leave a message for so-and-so, and if you say it right it gets passed along. Otherwise they never heard of the guy. Any club president can get on the phone and find any bro in the country in an hour, two hours tops. It works, and it's impossible for an outsider to tap into."

Benjamin shook his head. "There it is, Dennison. That's what we're up against."

"And now it's coming to a head."

Benjamin nodded. "So far the bikers' power—on a national level—has been diluted by the tension between the Outsiders in the West and the Mad Dogs in the East. But if the Outsiders can talk Apeman and the Mad Dogs into some kind of alliance, if they all start working together, the picture changes. They won't have to waste resources defending against each other. They'll have the manpower and money to move into territory that neither of them has taken over yet. They'll have a griplock on the whole country inside of three months."

"What about Rock?" Dennison asked. "Is he serious about a truce, or is that smokescreen?"

"Hard to say. Rock knows Apeman wants to take over the whole show. That means Apeman can't be trusted—but he can be manipulated. Rock may be able to make a peace treaty work at least temporarily—until he can get up enough muscle to double-cross Apeman."

"Then both of them have to be stopped now," Dennison said. "Before they can get together, before either becomes strong enough to take over the whole show. We've got to block the alliance, and break up the Outsiders and the Mad Dogs in the process.''

Dennison set his elbows on the desk and steepled his fingers. He was watching Charley Benjamin as if waiting for the answer to a question just posed. Benjamin looked away and squirmed in his chair.

Miss Paradise glanced quizzically at Dennison. Dennison nodded, almost imperceptibly.

''You're inside already,'' Miss Paradise said. Benjamin turned to her. ''Let's say we set up a divide-and-conquer operation. What can you do to help?'' She kept her voice neutral, nonjudgmental; like Dennison, she already had a notion of the answer.

''Not a goddamned thing.'' Benjamin's face paled. He stared at Dennison, as if pleading for help. For perhaps a half-minute neither man moved. Dennison said nothing, but Charley Benjamin had nothing to be ashamed of. The agent had done his job, and damned well.

''I'm scared, Dennison,'' he muttered. ''I am scared out of my goddamned mind.''

''What the hell?'' Miss Paradise said, startled and a little embarrassed for him.

Benjamin looked at her. ''You know those cracks I made when you came in?''

''Yeah. You're a hell of an actor.''

''It was no act.''

''What are you talking about?''

Benjamin shook his head helplessly. ''In a long-term deep-cover infiltration, you do not act. You live the part, twenty-four hours a day, every day of your life. Because if you don't—if you make one mistake, say one word that is out of character—you are dead. These bikers are scumbags, but they are not stupid. I had to be one of them—goddammit, I *was* one of them. I was Chicken Charley the Child Molester— and lately I was starting to lose my grip on Charles Benjamin.''

His hands were trembling. ''I can't hack it anymore,

20

Dennison. It's that simple. I'm stressed out. Someone else has got to take over." Benjamin pushed fingers through his greasy long hair and squared his shoulders. "Someone who can handle the job."

Benjamin took a deep breath. "That's you, Dennison," he said. "Will you do it?"

Dennison smiled. "You know the answer to that."

"We've got to infiltrate someone, and we don't have the time to finesse it too neatly. That makes it more dangerous." From near the open window Dennison could see across the side lawn of his compound, and down into the canyon through which the river ran, a couple of thousand feet below. Spring runoff was almost over, and Dennison had noticed over the last week that the sound of the water was down.

"What's the play?"

Dennison turned. Charley Benjamin had gone out to the front porch. Miss Paradise sat in Dennison's desk chair, hands clasped behind her neck.

"Put the Outsiders and the Mad Dogs at each other's throats," Dennison said. "Make them defeat each other."

"How?"

"Start a fight," Dennison said. "Pass false rumors. Cause a lot of trouble. Anything that will break up the alliance and damage the two controlling clubs."

"You make it sound easy, boss dear," Miss Paradise murmured.

Dennison turned. "It won't be. Count on that."

Miss Paradise drew her long lithe form out of the chair. "Then I'll call Chris Amado." She started for the office door.

Dennison gave her a narrow look and said nothing.

"Well, boss dear," Miss Paradise said finally, turning to face him. "You know how I like to try to think the way you do, 'cause you're my hero. Matt Conte is out: it wasn't so long ago he was working for the Mob, and according to our sources, the bikers are hooked in with the Mafia; there's too

21

much danger of someone recognizing Matt. Neither Price nor Vang fit the part; I can't see either of them as bikers, and neither will the bikers. Only two of our other people are the right age and have the right backgrounds for it. One of them broke a leg two days ago sliding into second base in a slow-pitch softball game, and the other is on a long-term surveillance."

"Which leaves Chris," Dennison said with forbearance.

"Shall I track her down?" Miss Paradise said.

"You do that, my dear," Dennison said.

BOOK ONE

The Velvet Glove

Chapter One

The bike was a Harley-Davidson Electra-Glide with a fatbob tank mounted on a frame raked at forty degrees, and chrome XA springers that extended a full four inches longer than stock. The radical modifications made the big machine look always ready to spring into motion, like a panther frozen before it leaped on prey. The pegs had been remounted so the rider's legs stretched out nearly horizontally. The legally required mirror was no bigger than a fifty-cent piece, the seat a leather pad the size of home plate. The front fender had been removed, the rear fender bobbed to the limit. When the cycle had left the factory on Juneau Street in Milwaukee, the 74-cubic-inch shovelhead engine had a larger displacement than some compact cars; since then it had been rebored for additional horsepower. This was a rig built for speed and distance, stripped of anything that did not contribute directly to functionality. The custom paint job was equally utilitarian, eight coats of silver-cloud metallic. The bike weighed slighty more than four hundred pounds.

The rider sat leaning slightly forward, hands glued to the gooseneck pull-back handlebars, helmetless, short dark hair whipped back in the slipstream, eyes studying the road as it reeled beneath the thinline Dunlop tires. The rider wore tight black leather slacks, black boots with straps across the tops, a sleeveless tank top that had been white once, a denim cutoff without club colors, and a black leather belt holding a sheathed Buck knife. The road was two-lane blacktop, cutting an arrow-straight scar across the featureless desert. Heat shimmered off to the right, toward flat-top buttes. Bike and rider moved at an even 100 mph.

The roadhouse was on California 58 a couple miles west of Barstow, a square squat cinder-block building with a swaybacked frame house attached in the back. It was called the Hellhole, and it looked to live up to the name. Behind the house was a four-stall garage, paint curling off the warped planks. The parking lot was hard-packed unpaved dirt, and at the edge near the road an unlit neon sign was fashioned in the shape of a devilkin holding a red pitchfork and grinning wickedly. There were a dozen bikes in the lot, all of them Harleys, and one windowless black panel truck.

Chris Amado downshifted the silver-cloud Electra-Glide and pulled in among the other bikes in the Hellhole's parking lot. In low gear and low throttle, the bike sounded like an ogre gargling.

Dennison's sources reported that the Hellhole was owned by the Outsiders and doubled as their southern California headquarters. In the legitimate businesses they owned, the biker gangs rarely put up much front. Places like the Hellhole were mean-enough-looking to keep out the casually curious, and most cops. Customers were superfluous; the Outsiders didn't make their money selling drinks over a bar. The Hellhole was a washing machine: dirty money from criminal operations went in, and clean money came out, to be passed through the books of the dummy corporation that legally owned the Hellhole.

The inside of the joint smelled of stale beer and greasy hamburgers. There were no windows; the crew in a place like this did not want to be reminded of sunshine, daylight, the real world. Most of the dim light came from the neon logos of a dozen brands of beer, hanging at random over the back bar and on the cinder-block walls. Budweiser lamps with plastic shades shaped like racks of billiard balls hung over the twin coin-operated pool tables.

Opposite the front door a bar ran the length of the room, fronted by a dozen stools; the vinyl seats on most of them were torn or slashed, and tufts of kapok sprouted from the gaps like an old man's chin whiskers. At one end of the bar was a little copse of six wooden-handled beer taps. On the back-bar shelf stood a couple dozen bottles of liquor and about the same number of glasses, and beside them was a stand-up double-wide glass-doored cooler crammed with frosted beer mugs. At the other end was a fry-grill, its surface black with generations of crusted burger fat, left unscraped to lubricate and flavor the next order. Two limp meat patties were sizzling there, their edges flapping helplessly, as if trying to call for help.

Chris Amado did not blame them. The Hellhole would not normally have been her first choice for a midday beer to wash the desert dust from her throat.

There were a dozen bikers in the place, all of them in dirty jeans and cutoffs and long matted hair, all but a couple bearded, all Outsiders. As her eyes got used to the dimness, Chris could make out the Outsider patch on the backs of the sleeveless jackets: a macabre stylized death's-head skull, grinning madly above crossed long-barrel hogleg revolvers, their muzzles dribbling smoke. Some of the bikers sat at a couple of the eight or nine round tables scattered around the unscrubbed wooden floor, a litter of beer mugs and overflowing ashtrays in front of them; Chris noticed the sweeter smell of marijuana cutting the rank cooking odor. Another was at the bar, negotiating another round. One guy was lining up a bank shot at the pool table, and his buddy was leaning against the wall under a black-velvet painting of a pendulous-breasted blond fingering herself. Opposite him, a skinny kid with bad teeth stood at a jukebox, his fingers poised over the selection buttons.

Everyone seemed frozen, as if the place were caught in a warp in the fabric of time. Every biker in the place had stopped what he was doing to stare at Chris, standing just inside the door. Here was a challenge, palpable as a child's boasting dare.

That was fine. That was what she was here for.

Chris moved across the room, studiously casual, letting them get a good look. She wore no bra; the sleeveless tank top was tight enough to leave no doubt about that. She met pairs of eyes long enough to return the challenge, deliberately put her back to all of them when she slid up on a bar stool.

"What the fuck do you want?"

The bartender was a tall dishwater blond, the only other woman in the room. She wore her hair in a bun pinned up on top of her head, and her oversized breasts strained against a white T-shirt decorated with the green Bardahl logo. She could have been pretty, except her face was too hard-edged, chiseled into a permanent defensive suspicious glare. This was the face of a woman who had endured a good deal of life and found it mostly unpleasant.

"That's a new one," Chris said. "I've been in plenty of cribs, heard lots of opening lines from bartenders. Mostly 'What'll it be?', 'What's a chick like you doing here?', once in a while some kind of half-dirty come-on. But never 'What the fuck do you want?' That's different." She gave the bartender a cold hard smile that had nothing to do with companionability. "I like that a lot."

"You're making a big mistake."

"Yeah," Chris said, suddenly bored. "So give me a brew."

The blond's mouth slammed shut like a screen door. Behind Chris someone muttered something too low for her to hear, and someone else laughed. The laughter was aimed in her direction, like a thin stream of icy water; she could feel it ripple over her back.

The bartender slapped a mug in front of her, deliberately slopping beer on the bar. "Buck," she said. Chris laid a one-dollar bill in the puddle of beer, smiled, and said, "Keep the change, sweetie."

The blond looked at the money like it was a turd. "Listen, honeybuns," she said. "If you want to pull the train for about two dozen dudes, you are in the right place." But then her eyes narrowed, and for the first time something approaching shrewdness came into them. "Only you don't look like anyone's mama." She shook her head. "Doesn't matter. Drink up and get out. You got no business here."

Chris picked up the mug and tipped it back, drank until it was empty. She set it down, slid it toward the blond. " 'Nother."

"What do you want here?"

"Another brew. If I can get one."

Chris waited until the big blond set the refill in front of her and was reaching for the money, then said offhandedly, "Is Rock around?"

The woman's hand froze, the dollar bill speared between two overlong red-enameled fingernails. The mindless hostility left her expression and was replaced by something more seriously lethal. "What do you want with Rock?" Her voice was a low hiss.

"Just round him up, sweetie," Chris said. "I'll mind the store while you're gone."

The bartender seemed to shake for a moment with cold fury. She opened her mouth to speak, and Chris turned deliberately away. A biker had slid onto the stool to her left. His black beard did not completely hide the pockmarks that dappled his skin, mementos of a violent long-ago losing battle with acne. He was shirtless under his cutoff, and his beer gut was big enough to hide most of the polished chain drive he wore as a belt. His teeth, when he grinned, were the color of mahogany. The blond bartender drew a beer and slid it in front of him without being asked.

The fat biker grinned at his bros as if he were performing for them or had a bet on. The others grinned back, licked unconsciously at their lips. They knew what came next. They had seen this before, but it was always a treat, like a favorite golden oldie heard late at night on the radio. Someone sucked noisily on a joint and said, "That goddamned Grotty is one classy dude." He was trying to hold the smoke in, and his voice was tight and strained, and ripe with anticipation.

One pair of bikers at a corner table caught Chris's eye, because they made such an odd couple. The big guy was easily the best-looking dude in the room; he looked more like a surfer than a biker, with long wavy blond hair and clean-cut beach-boy features tanned a uniform bronze. His partner looked like a rodent. He was so short, probably only a few inches over five feet, that when he was sitting down the tabletop came up to his chest, like a small child. His wispy black beard was too thin to disguise his chinless jaw, and his overbite was as prominent as a woodchuck's. The blond guy was watching her like everyone else, but shrewdly, like a USDA inspector grading a hog carcass. The rodent watched the blond guy watch her. He looked confused.

The fat biker to Chris's left drained half his beer and wiped his beard with the back of his hand. "You're looking lonely, woofie."

"I'm not lonely," Chris said. "And I'm not a woofie."

The biker was still grinning, but his voice turned cold. "You could be." He inclined his head toward the rest of the room. "Nothing the bros like better'n strange ginch. Like the man says, variety is the spice of life. I say the word, and you are turned out. You'll get the goddamned ride of your life, bitch." The biker shrugged elaborately. " 'Course, some chicks like that, can't get enough cock, take it everywhere it'll fit and a couple of places it normally won't. You must be that kind, huh?"

There was nothing about this Chris liked, because the dirtbag son of a bitch was right. This whole scene was a hair-trigger pull from blowing up, and if it did, she was at ground zero.

"What kind is that?" she said levelly.

"Someone who needs a friend—like Grotty."

Chris looked him up and down. "Grotty?"

"I'm Grotty." The biker poked himself in his bare flabby chest and looked genuinely proud, like a retiree who'd just been presented his engraved gold watch.

"Yeah," Chris drawled, loud enough for everyone to hear. "You're about the grottiest piece of garbage I've seen in a month."

Someone snickered. Grotty's face darkened. Chris shot a glance at the bartender. The blond woman was smiling with grim satisfaction; she was going to enjoy seeing this stuck-up bitch get what she was begging for.

Grotty grabbed Chris's left arm above the elbow, hard fingers digging into her bicep. The bastard may have had a beer gut, but biking favored the arms and shoulders, and he was strong enough to hurt her—and outweighed her about two to one.

"You listen good, mama." Flecks of beery spittle flew from his mouth. "You got maybe one chance of getting out of here without having about a dozen dicks rammed into every hole you got. We're making it, you and me. You see that pool table?"

"Where?" Chris said.

The biker frowned, then cocked his head at it.

Chris slammed her half-full mug of beer into the middle of the guy's face. The heavy glass did not shatter, but the biker's nose did. He yowled and slapped both hands over it, blood streaming between his cupped fingers. Chris rabbit-punched him with a double fist at the base of his skull and the guy tumbled off the stool, withdrawing instinctively into a fetal curl, muscle memory recalling the last time he'd been stomped.

Chris drove the toe of her boot into his face, and when he covered it with his arms, she kicked him twice in the rib cage, hard enough to crack bone.

Grotty stopped moaning or moving. The fight had lasted maybe eight seconds.

"Son of a bitch," someone said, with equal portions of surprise, anger, and admiration.

"Look what she done."

"The cunt stomped our bro."

The guy at the pool table picked up a cue by the thin end and clubbed it. "Fuck if she's a chick. She stomped Grotty."

"Get the bitch!"

Chris reached around to the holster riding under the cutoffs at the small of her back and took out a COP 2+2 derringer. She put her back to the bar and leveled the little gun on the guy with the pool cue.

"I've got four barrels here," she said, as if delivering a lecture. "Each one is holding 125 grains of hollow-point .357 Magnum lead. A load like that will make a hole in your gut big enough to drive a Honda through—even fat pigs like you." Chris shrugged elaborately. "After a while the rest of you get to stomp me, yeah—but the four of you I'm going to take out are going to be dead meat." She waggled the gun at the guy with the cue. "You're first, freakshow, unless you put that stick down pronto."

For a moment the guy did not move. Then he laid the cue on the felt, gently, as if it might explode if jarred. He was grinning, and looking past Chris.

Chris stepped away from the bar and turned the COP on the big blond bartender. The woman paled and lowered the whiskey bottle she held by the neck over her head.

"I'm going to save the last one for you, bitch," Chris snapped. "I'll blow your fucking tits off."

At the far table a guy stood, moving carefully and keeping his hands in sight. Chris had not noticed him before. He was tall, sandy-haired, and his stomach was flat and girded with muscle. He gave Chris a tolerant smile, as if this were the sort of misunderstanding that could be worked out between reasonable adults. He was clean-shaven, and not bad-looking.

"What now, princess?" he said, casually as the time of day.

"I'm looking for Rock, bro," Chris said.

"All right," the guy said pleasantly. "Let's go see Rock."

Chapter Two

The door at the far end of the bar opened into a hallway stretching into the bowels of the frame house Chris had seen when she pulled into the Hellhole parking lot. Two unshaded low-wattage bulbs threw jaundiced light that failed to reach into the dim corners. The sandy-haired biker shut the door, then turned so he was blocking the corridor. He grinned, not unpleasantly. He wasn't quite as rank as the other Outsiders, although he would have stood out at a Chamber of Commerce breakfast.

"What say you give me the piece, princess?"

Chris still held the little .357 in her right hand, but loosely, the four barrels pointing at the floor between them. "Uh-uh."

The sandy-haired biker looked down at one of the brass buttons on his cutoff, and began toying with it absently. "You see how it is, princess," he said reasonably. "I can't take you in to see Rock if you're heeled. A guy like Rock makes enemies."

"I wonder why." She brought up the gun. "Now, let's see to business."

The biker shook his head. "You ain't gonna shoot me, not unless you are tired of living yourself. The only way out of here is back through the bar, and you wouldn't get three steps." He plucked at the button, looking unsure, as if he were not accustomed to reasoning with a woman.

"Just the same," Chris said, "you don't get the piece."

The sandy-haired biker shrugged—and the hand at the button shot out and clipped Chris under the chin. As her head went back, she felt the derringer evaporate from her hand. Her legs did not work exactly right, and drifting storm clouds made it difficult to see in the hallway's twilight. A hand clamped around her wrist.

"Let's call that one even-up for Grotty," the biker's voice said. "See you around, princess."

The plane of the floor tilted and came up and hit her in the back of the head. A door slammed. Getting up seemed a remote possibility, and before she could try it the clouds thickened to a uniform blackness.

Chris Amado had been a warrior for most of her adult life. She was not a thrill-seeker, had no pathological need for risk or violence. She fought from a sense of responsibility; she fought because someone had to face the Beast.

She was a U.S. citizen, born in Ithaca, New York, but she grew up in Santa Cruz, a small agricultural nation on the northeastern coast of South America. Her father Rafael was native-born; her mother, Elizabeth, a member of a prominent family in Old Lyme, Connecticut. They met and married at Cornell, where Rafael Amado was studying agricultural science, and when they graduated they returned to Santa Cruz with their new baby.

Chris was back in the United States, in her second year at Harvard, when her father was murdered. By then he was minister of agriculture in his native country. He had prepared a sweeping program of agricultural reform that would do away with the feudal system of farming under which five percent of the population of Santa Cruz owned ninety percent of the land, a system under which field hands worked for pennies an hour, a lean-to hut, and no chance of ever achieving better. Rafael Amado's plan would compensate big landowners while giving equal opportunities to everyone; it was a system where ambition, thrift, and honest labor—not birthright—were the keys to success and its rewards.

It was a brilliant reform package, and it would have worked, if Rafael Amado had not been assassinated by an Army lieutenant during the military coup that rocked the nation and left thousands of Santa Cruz civilians dead. Within days the generals controlled the government, and Santa Cruz wriggled impotently in their chain-mail grip.

The peasants of Santa Cruz had neither the money nor the weapons to mount a full-scale counterrevolutionary effort, but some of them organized to mount guerrilla actions to harass, embarrass, and weaken the generals. The guerrillas called themselves Amadistas, after the man who had designed the reform. When they went into the jungle, Chris Amado went with them.

For the next nine years she fought as an Amadista. The generals had the guns, the troops, and the seat of power. The Amadistas had the fervent dedication of people who had been robbed of everything they owned, and who were now being hunted like animals.

As the long war ground on, Chris Amado's role grew. She continued to participate in covert jungle actions, but she also became a representative of the Amadistas, serving as liaison with other people's groups in Latin America, raising money, weapons, and awareness.

By the time she was thirty, four Central American countries had joined Santa Cruz in offering ten thousand dollars for Chris Amado or her corpse.

She protested against abandoning the cause, but the other Amadista leaders insisted she had no choice. She was a symbol of the movement; her capture or murder would be a devastating blow to morale. For the time being, she had to leave the area. It was decided she would return to the United

States on a fund-raising mission, meeting with groups sympathetic to the fight for human rights.

She made it as far as Mexico City.

The corrupt official who planted the cocaine on her was named Enrico. He was in no hurry to turn her over to the generals for the reward; he had other uses for her while he dickered with the generals over price. For the next nine months she lived in filth and degradation in a hellhole stone-and-iron dungeon. About once a month she was taken to Enrico's home, where the fat greasy pig raped her. She was half *gringa;* that turned Enrico on.

Years in the jungle had taught her survival, and she determined from the day the cell door clanked shut that she would live through this and come out strong as ever. She forced herself to remain alert to any chance.

Chance appeared in the form of a neat, compact Oriental man with a submachine gun one night when she was in Enrico's bed. The timing was excellent. She had just caved in Enrico's skull with a brass candlestick.

The Oriental man's name was Vang, and he took her to Dennison. Chris had never heard of Dennison—few people had—but he knew of her. Dennison needed her help. He ran a network of professional fighters, men and women who handled the jobs conventional agencies could not, warriors concerned with ends not means, with results not rules. Dennison's Warriors were the best, and were paid well; it was a chance to earn a lot of money quickly for the Amadista cause.

Chris accepted Dennison's offer on those terms, but she soon learned that the money was secondary; Dennison and his Warriors had more immediate concerns. Chris had been totally immersed in the Santa Cruz revolution for so long, she had forgotten about the rest of the world. It was going to hell, Dennison reminded her. He didn't expect to set the world instantly right—but he was damned if he was going to do nothing. The jackals were on the prowl, and it wasn't enough to lock and barricade the door.

Occasionally you had to exterminate a few of the beasts.

The world has gone wrong, Dennison told her—but we get even.

Chris realized that she and Dennison had been fighting the same war for a long time. For the time being she was out of the game in Santa Cruz, but Dennison was giving her a chance to keep up the fight, to crush a few of the parasites who sucked the life from the good people of the world.

Chris Amado had stalked the killing ground long enough to know she'd take some lumps. In the Santa Cruz jungle she had been knocked out, and she had been shot. Knocked out was better—but, Chris thought as she painfully raised her head from the floor of the dank room behind the Hellhole, it was never a whole lot of fun.

Her jaw was sore, and eating was going to hurt for a day or two, but everything moved the way it was supposed to, so nothing was broken. There was a soft damp swollen spot on the back of her head, but her vision was normal and her headache bearable. The gun, of course, was gone, and the leather sheath on her belt was empty of the Buck knife.

She was not wearing a watch—bikers ran on their own erratic schedule, and had little use for "citizen time"—but instinct told her she had been out only a few minutes. She dragged herself to her feet, using a hand on the wall to steady herself. She closed her eyes, drew breath, exhaled, and listened to her own pulse rate. By the time it was normal she was able to stand by herself.

She was locked up in what she guessed was the Outsiders' turn-out room, the place set aside for mamas or strange chicks who wanted—or were forced—to get friendly with the bros. In his briefing, Charley Benjamin had explained to her that among outlaw bikers, sex rarely had anything to do with pleasure. Bikers used sex as dominance, a way to hurt or punish someone.

The exceptions were the old ladies; an old lady was a woman married to or going with one of the bikers. An old lady belonged to one bro only, and messing with someone's old lady was a stomping offense. Of course, in a case like that the old lady would probably be stomped as well. A woman was a possession; according to Benjamin, a Salt Lake City club made it a practice to tattoo "Property of the Black Dukes" on their old ladies' rumps.

Mamas were the biker groupies, women who hung out at the club's bar or headquarters and put out for anyone who wanted a quick tumble. These were sad, often disturbed young women with a pathetic need for abuse. On one run, Charley Benjamin told her, he had seen a bro trade a mama for a tank of gas. On another, a club raffled off a shot at one of its mamas to raise beer money. The winning bid was forty-seven cents.

A "strange chick" was any woman who wandered in and put out—and that was the category Chris would find herself in if she didn't play the next few hours very damned coolly.

The turn-out room stank of the more rank human functions. One half of the floor was covered with bare mattresses and a variety of discolored pillows and cushions; the plank floor, where it showed, was sticky with dried beer and littered with crushed cigarette butts. In one corner there was an empty dented beer keg, in another a pile of discarded bras and panties. The walls were decorated with pictures torn from magazines and taped up at random: slack-breasted women with fingers hidden between open legs, or joylessly coupling with a man, or two men, or each other.

Chris Amado leaned against the wall facing the door and worked at taking shallow breaths through her mouth.

She guessed that two hours passed before the door opened. The sandy-haired biker crossed his arms and showed her his open grin. "Did I hurt you, princess?"

Chris let that one pass.

"Been talking about you to Rock," the guy said. "I told him how you did Grotty, and how foxy you look. 'Course Rock don't have much interest in stray suckies since Lizzie

38

become his old lady." He took a cigarette from behind his ear and looked it over. "I don't think Lizzie likes you, princess."

"The bartender with the sloppy tits?"

The biker nodded. "You know why they call her Lizzie?"

"Yeah," Chris said. "It's short for 'dyke.'"

The biker laughed. "Close. It's short for 'Lizard Tongue.' That's what the bros used to call her, anyway the ones who got a taste before Rock put his brand on her."

Chris suppressed a shudder. She had a feeling the part about the brand was literal.

"Let's do some business," the biker said.

Chris followed him down the corridor and through the second door to the right, into the bar's storeroom. A cooler ran along one wall, and there were stacks of cases of beer nuts, cigarettes, hamburger buns, along with several dozen empty kegs. A man sat on one of them and stared at Chris.

"Where's my goddamned knife?" she said.

The man on the keg regarded her.

"You took my piece," Chris said. "All right, I can live with that for the time being. But you do not take a bro's knife."

The man called Rock had the slight wiry build of a dancer or a gymnast; Chris had the impression of someone who deliberated his options, then moved with cobra quickness. His hair was obsidian black and combed straight back, as if permanently coiffed by a lifetime of hard biking; it was cut a little below his collar, and was almost clean. Like Snake, the sandy-haired one, he was clean-shaven, and the angles of his deeply tanned face were sharply etched as a granite cliff. He wore very dark shades in teardrop aviator frames. The lenses completely obscured his eyes, so his face looked disquietingly alien, almost reptilian; his eyes were the focus of a constant restrained menace. He held a thick white cup of black coffee.

Chris put Rock's age at somewhere between thirty and forty; the dark glasses made it hard to pin down. He wore the biker uniform of boots, jeans, and cutoff over a plain black

T-shirt. On his hip was a .45 Peacemaker revolver with a ten-inch barrel, the single-action gunfighter piece that Colt had been making since the days of Wyatt Earp and Wild Bill Hickok. He wore the holster low-slung, the tip tied down by a rawhide thong around his thigh above the knee.

"Snake here says you stomped Grotty." Rock sipped at his coffee. "You say you claim to be a bro." He shook his head, as if that presented complex conflicts of major import. "What's your name?"

"Tell him your name, princess," Snake said.

Chris gave him a grin. "Princess—I like that. It'll do for now."

Rock's fingers were long, tapered, clean, and uncallused. This was not a man who had to fix his own scoot. "You hurt Grotty pretty bad," he said. "He's in the hospital, surrounded by croakers and straight citizens. One of the ribs you broke stuck him in the lung."

"Good thing he has a spare," Chris said.

"Trouble is," Rock said, "Grotty is an Outsider. You stomped our bro." His tone was patient, logical; facts were facts, rules were rules. "What we're going to do, I think, is take you back out to the bar and strip off those leathers, and then the bros will do you. After that, we'll load you into the back of that panel truck out front, drive you maybe a hundred miles out in the desert, beat hell out of you, and set you afoot. No food, no water, no clothes, no friends . . ."

". . . and no chance," Snake finished.

They could do it—and Chris had no doubt that they would, unless she could give them a good reason not to. "You'd be making a big mistake."

Rock sipped at his coffee and waited for her to go on. Here was a studiously cautious man.

"You'd be turning down a bro on the run."

"What do you want?"

"A place to stay. Some protection."

"This ain't the Salvation Army Mission, Princess," Snake said.

"Look," Chris said patiently. "I rode with the Black Aces out of Grant's Pass. I was a prospect."

"A wannabee." Snake sneered.

Chris ignored him "There was some trouble."

"With the Black Aces?"

"With the law. I had to run a job to get in. You know how it is." To assure that a newcomer wasn't an undercover cop, Benjamin had said, clubs demanded that the wannabee commit a felony before being granted full membership. "I was delivering a pound of crystal meth to a guy in Eugene. It was a setup—the cops had turned the bastard. They were waiting for me."

"So?"

"So I shot a cop."

"Dead?"

"In the knee."

Snake nodded with something like approval. You did not kill a cop unless you had to. You could beat the rap, but it wasn't worth the hassle.

"What were you before that, Princess? Before you started running meth for the Aces?"

"A citizen," Chris snapped. You did not ask a bro what he did before, in his righteous life.

"Check her out," Snake suggested.

Rock put down his coffee cup and went to the wall phone near the door. Chris watched him unscrew the mouthpiece and replace it with a thick screw-on device with three buttons and a pilot light on the side. *Bug-sweeper*, Chris thought—but there was nothing she could do about that now. "You got a smoke?" Chris said to Snake. He hesitated, then pulled a pack of Camels from the pocket of his cutoff and passed it over. Chris lit up. Rock was asking the person on the other end of the phone if he'd seen Chuck the Duck lately.

In the time it took Chris to smoke the cigarette, Rock

made three more calls. She smiled at Snake and pretended not to pay attention. Behind her, Rock said into the phone, "Hey there, bro. What's happening?"

Chris ground the butt into the floorboards.

Rock said into the phone, "I got a chick here who calls herself Princess. Says she ran into some bad blue running a delivery for you."

Chris looked up into Snake's smirk and shook her head, as if he ought to know better.

On the phone, Rock said, "Yeah, bro, much obliged. Later." The receiver clicked on the hook.

Rock drank from the coffee cup and stared at her thoughtfully. No part of his face moved, and the dark shades were like two bottomless holes in his skull. "Okay, Princess," he said finally. "What do you want?"

Chris shot him a cocky grin. "For starters," she said, "you can give me back my goddamned piece."

William Sterling Price flicked the cutoff switch, removed the headphones, and pushed his swivel chair away from the communication console that ran along one side wall of the GMC motor home. Desert sunlight filtered through the tinted glass of the back-door windows and the skylight.

Vang stood behind a second chair opposite the console. He and Price had been with Dennison since soon after the fall of Saigon. Price had been a colonel of the Green Berets, Vang the commander of the Hmong warriors who had fought with such distinction and valor for the U.S. in the Laotian highlands around the Plain of Jars.

Chuck the Duck sat in the chair, his face greasy with sweat and anger. He hiked at his cutoff and scowled at Price.

"You did a good job, scumbag," Price said.

"You bastards are in a lot of trouble. You kidnapped me and you took me across a state line. That's a federal rap. I know my rights."

"You've got no rights. You are walking on glass. If we

want to, we can put you on the kind of ice where you'll never defrost."

Uncertainty flashed across Chuck's slick face. "You turn me over and you're in shit deep as I am," he blustered.

Price looked at Vang and shrugged.

"Sure." Chuck's confidence was returning. "You got no choice except to let me loose." He blossomed into a huge insolent grin. "And as soon as you do, you are dead. Both you bastards are history. You'll want your back to the wall at all times, because I am going to get you assholes."

"No you won't," Price said evenly. "You've already forgotten you ever ran into us." Price leaned over the biker. "If Rock calls you on this, you don't know a damned thing. Someone set you up, imitated your voice."

"Like hell."

"You forgot one thing, scumbag: you sold out. You finked on your bros. If you try coming back on us, or even talk about it, we'll put the word out—and you'll be feeding the buzzards, scumbag."

The biker stared up at Price. Anger mottled his pale complexion like a rash. "You cocksucker," he snarled, and started out of the chair.

Vang clamped his thumb and forefinger around the base of his neck, and the biker's face contorted with pain. Price leaned close to Chuck. "I am about this far from walking all over your face, asshole. Get smart."

Chuck opened his mouth to speak, and Vang increased the pressure. The biker's eyes closed and he went limp in the chair.

Price straightened and nodded at Vang. "Let's get rid of this cockroach," he said.

Vang looked at his hand and grimaced, as if it were smeared with something distasteful. "As quickly as possible," he agreed. "I forgot to get my shots."

43

Chapter Three

Chris Amado felt the roar of the huge 74-cubic-inch engine between her legs, its throbbing power almost animate. The high summer sun was warm on her bare arms, and the landscape whipped past like an endless movie projected at triple speed. She felt invigorated and alive.

She understood the cyclist's thrill. On the racing Harley, a rider was alone at the center of a private universe. It took strength and steady nerve and a fair portion of raw guts to pilot the big bike; it took someone who needed risk like nourishment. A bike was freedom, control, mastery. With a bike you could be anywhere, anytime; you had to pity the citizens, the four-wheelers who built their own cages and locked themselves in.

The afternoon before, in the storeroom in the back of the Hellhole outside of Barstow, Rock had looked at her through the opaque black lenses of his shades and said, "Why do I still have the idea that you could be a cop, Princess?"

Chris snorted and shook her head in disgust.

"Far as I know, cops don't walk into a joint and stomp someone," Snake said thoughtfully. " 'Course they may have changed that rule without telling us."

"I could use a brew," Chris said.

Rock examined his coffee cup. "If she wants in, she pulls a job like any other wannabee."

"I thought Chuck the Duck filled you in," Chris said. "Remember, there are some dudes with badges up in the Bay Area who'd like to talk to me about a pound of crystal and a cop with a shot-up knee."

"That's Black Ace business, Princess," Snake said.

"You want to ride with the Outsiders," Rock said. "You want protection. So you do something for us in return."

"Look," Chris said reasonably, "if I have to do a job, I'll do a job. I'll knock over the goddamned Federal Reserve Bank in Denver if you'd like. Only for right now," Chris said, "can I have a fucking beer?"

Rock stared for a moment, then laughed. "Sure, Princess. I'll buy."

For the rest of the afternoon and into the evening, she sipped beer and pretended to become progressively drunker. Rock stuck around long enough to tell her to be ready to ride the next morning. He gave her no details of the job, and Chris did not waste time asking. She would have to play it by ear.

She could handle the improvisation part; for a decade her survival had depended on quick thinking and quicker action. A greater concern was that this part of the operation had to run out in the open, among the public and citizens and innocent bystanders. The odds for unexpected trouble doubled or tripled when there were civilians around.

Vang and Price were covering her, so far without any trouble. If they hadn't been on the job, the phone call to Chuck the Duck would have ripped her cover off. But if anything went wrong on the run, she'd be on her own. The action would go down hard and fast, and if the unanticipated happened, she'd have seconds to decide whether to risk her cover—and her life—or watch some amateur do-gooder get shot up in the crossfire.

Rock was another concern. The Outsider president must have been a typical biker once, but he seemed to have risen above that. In the barroom he continued to drink coffee instead of beer; that was as gauche as showing up for a run on a moped. As soon as he finished talking with her, he left and did not return, as if he had a low tolerance for suds-swilling and the accompanying high jinks. His attitude toward the others bordered on contempt, yet he commanded their respect, even deference. Chris shared that respect; she tabbed Rock as shrewd and potentially lethal.

As soon as Rock left, Lizzie stalked down to where Chris sat. Lizzie leaned over so her face was close to Chris's and her big breasts rested on the bar. "You better understand how it is, honey," she said in a low hard voice.

"How is it?" Chris sipped at her beer.

"I'm Queen Bitch in this club. You keep that in mind, and out of my way. Rock is my man."

It was an opportunity to exploit, Chris decided. If the idea was to cause dissension in the biker ranks, Lizzie was playing right into it.

"Is that so?" she said offhandedly.

Lizzie's hard face darkened. "What's that mean?"

"Figure it out."

Lizzie's eyes narrowed with an inkling of understanding. "What were you and Rock doing in the back room?"

"What you think." Chris took another drink.

"You fucking cunt!" Lizzie screamed, and clawed for Chris.

Chris spewed a mouthful of beer into her face. It dripped off her chin and nose and the ends of her brassy blond hair. For a moment Lizzie froze in rage and disbelief.

She grabbed for Chris's face again, and Chris caught her wrist in midair and twisted. Lizzie grunted with pain. Chris started to twist harder.

"That's enough."

Snake was beside her at the bar. "Let her go."

Slowly Chris released Lizzie's arm. Her smoldering eyes were glistening with tears of pain. "I'll get you for this, you goddamned whore bitch."

"You and me," Chris said. "Anytime you want."

"Go wash your face, Lizzie," Snake said. He watched her go out the back door before turning to Chris again. "You do like to fight."

Chris gave him a tight grin. "I'm a biker, bro."

It was enough for the first night. Trouble was already piling up at a good clip, and there would surely be more on the next day's run.

*   *   *

Snake was in charge, and a biker called Crazy George was riding beside him. George had haunted bloodshot eyes sunk deep in their sockets, and whenever Snake called a pit stop, George loaded both nostrils with a snort of speed. He was skeletally thin, and he chattered constantly, muttering to himself when no one else would listen, like a neglected child with an imaginary playmate.

The guy riding on Chris's right was Zippo. Zippo was a knife man. He carried a whetstone in a pouch on his belt next to his sheathed Buck; he liked to rehone the blade, he told her, after each time he used it. There was a crisscross of scars on his left arm from wrist to shoulder. Late at night, when the beer and Seconals and meth began to work their polypharmacological magic, Zippo sometimes liked to experiment with the knife on himself.

The Nevada desert was a monotonous plain of sparse sagebrush and monolithic granite upthrust buttes. The slip-stream at 100 mph felt as hot as the draft from an open furnace. A dozen miles north of Alamo, they turned off U.S. 93 onto the Nevada 38 cutoff. In the hour it took to cover the next 110 miles of nothingness, they passed one beat-up flatbed hauling bricks, a semi-rig making up sack time at a steady 80, two cars heading south, and three jackrabbits.

At the junction where 38 hit U.S. 6, Snake raised his left hand, palm forward, to signal a stop. They pulled into a gas station that looked like it had fallen asleep in 1940 and awakened that morning. The two pumps had round shoulders and circular heads; one was labeled "Regular," the other "Ethyl." The garage was a wood-frame building with a tiny office and two service bays. A faded red-lettered sign on the window glass read "Esso."

A white-haired man in dirty denim coveralls limped out of the office. "Help you folks?" he said, without enthusiasm.

"We'll pump, Pops," Snake said.

The old man nodded, as if that suited him just dandy, and turned back to the relative safety of the office.

"You got any beer, Pops?" Snake called.

The old man reluctantly looked at him. "In that icebox in the office. Five dollars a six-pack, sonny."

Snake smiled. "Didn't quite catch that, Pops."

"Take it or leave it, sonny. It's all the same to me."

Snake sauntered across the apron and stood over the old man. "Pops, how would you like me to tear you a new asshole?"

"Might as well. The one I got don't work a goddamn."

Chris braced for trouble—but then Snake shook his head and laughed. "You got balls, Pops." He peeled off a five-dollar bill from a good-sized roll. "But I bet you don't get to use them much these days."

A black GMC motor home pulled off the highway and coasted to a stop at the far end of the lot. The old man squinted at it with something like resentment. "You'd be surprised, sonny," he said to Snake. "Now, come get your brew." The old man limped toward the office. "Used to have me one of them scoots myself, before the war. An Indian Chief, stripped down slick as snot. Run one of them Harley hogs of yours into the ground, sonny."

Chris had topped off her fatbob tank by the time Snake returned with the six-pack. Crazy George yanked a can from the plastic collar, pulled the tab and tossed it over his shoulder, and drained the beer in one long slug. When he was finished and had caught his breath, he went back to his mumbling. Chris accepted a can and took a drink. The beer was good; it was damned good after the long hot ride.

Snake sat on his haunches and looked up at the other three. "You ever been to Ely, Princess?"

Chris shook her head.

"You're lucky. You make a list of jerkwater towns, Ely would be at the top. That's where we're heading. 'Bout twenty-five miles on down the road."

At the edge of the lot, the black van's motor started up.

Crazy George and Zippo stared vaguely at it. Whatever Snake had to say, they'd already heard.

"There's a place on the other side of Ely called McKay's Quik-Stop—grocery store, lunch counter, couple of gas pumps. This McKay dude was a cop in Brooklyn, put in his twenty years and took his pension, bought the Ely joint. He's also got a dozen slot machines."

"So?"

"So the Vegas boys control the slots south of I-80. Always have. McKay has got a problem with that. He's got some half-ass ideas about free enterprise and all that shit." Snake laughed. "I don't know what he's bitching about. The Vegas boys supply the machines, maintain them, set the odds—that's a lot of service for only two-thirds of the take. The Vegas boys have tried to reason with him, but he won't listen. This McKay dude walked a beat in the Big Apple, and he thinks that makes him king-shit."

"He ain't so tough," Crazy George put in.

"He won't be," Snake said. "Not after today."

The black van pulled to the edge of the road, waited for a stock truck to pass, and pulled out, heading east.

"George is the outside man," Snake said. "The rest of us'll visit with McKay."

"And do what?" Chris said.

"Just follow the leader, Princess. Are you heeled?"

"Sure."

"Then you got nothing to worry about."

A Winnebago turned into the service station and lumbered up to the pumps. A balding man in Bermuda shorts and a polo shirt climbed out and stared warily at the four of them, then gave all his attention to pumping gas. A boy of ten or eleven came around the front of the rig, followed by a toothy adolescent girl in a halter top. "Daddy," the girl said quietly. Her eyes were glued to the four bikers.

"Get back inside, Jennifer," the bald man muttered, not looking up.

"Yeah," Zippo said, loud enough for everyone to hear. "Get back inside, Jennifer—and take me with you."

"Hey, Jennifer," Crazy George rapped. "You ever seen a one-eyed snake?"

The bald man jerked erect as if someone had pulled his string. "Listen, you . . ."

Chris started to say something, but then Crazy George whooped and launched himself into Zippo's arms. Zippo caught him, and George planted a huge wet one on Zippo's lips. He disentangled himself and laid a kiss on Snake, who tolerated it with wry amusement, and then George hit Chris, hard enough to knock her over if he'd not been so skinny. Chris returned the kiss; it was an old biker gross-out for showing class in front of straight citizens.

The only thing that worried her was the wire-pack taped to her stomach under her T-shirt—and whether George would feel it.

But George was checking out the cagers. The kisses had the desired effect: the children were staring at them with fascination, the father with horror and loathing. The old geezer who owned the station was getting a huge kick out of all this. He dropped into a chair near the office door, chortling and slapping at his knee as if trying to revive vaudeville.

Snake chuckled indulgently. He rose up, kick-started his bike, and cranked the accelerator. The father tried to say something but the engine's whine drowned him out, and his mouth flapped impotent as a mute's.

Snake popped the clutch and his bike reared up in a wheelie for a good fifteen yards, dual pipes scorching the packed dirt of the station's apron. Chris came down on her own starter and was after him before the dust began to drift with the breeze.

McKay's Quik-Stop lacked the reassuringly sleek sameness of the chain stores; it had not been remodeled for a decade. There was a six-stool lunch counter, a half-dozen upright coolers full of beer, a paperback-book rack, a few shelves of potato chips and Hostess Twinkies and motor oil. The twelve slot machines were lined up in an L along the corner behind the front door.

McKay was behind the lunch counter, a big broad-shouldered man whose gut had begun to go soft since he'd retired from the force. He had a full head of graying hair, a bushy salt-and-pepper mustache, horn-rimmed glasses, and a deeply creased face.

He took a couple of steps along the counter toward them when they came in, and his eyes narrowed. Chris hung back near the door, waiting to see how the play developed. Out front on the apron, the same black GMC they had seen a half-hour earlier pulled up alongside the gas pumps.

Snake crossed to the counter and leered at McKay. Zippo stood a step behind him. The livid knife scars on his arm were crawling like worms; he was twitching with anticipation of imminent violence.

McKay set both palms flat on the counter. "What do you want?"

"Beats me." Snake looked at Zippo. "How about some Doritos?"

The wire rack of chips was at the end of a set of shelves. Zippo grabbed it by the top and dumped it over. He kicked the rack aside and stomped his boot down in the middle of the pile of cellophane bags. The crunching sound made him smile.

"Get out of here." McKay's voice was tight.

"Sure," Snake said. "Soon as we're finished." He grabbed a fistful of McKay's T-shirt. There were sweat stains under the older man's arms.

Chris slipped the COP .357 out of its belt holster and held it on the two of them.

"We're here about the slots, asshole," Snake said.

McKay tried to grab his arm.

Snake moved a step back and drew a .38 snub-nosed

51

Police Special from the back of his waistband, graceful as a ghost. He shot a quick glance over his shoulder and nodded approval when he saw that Chris was already covering McKay.

"Do it, Zippo," Snake said softly. "Don't bust up any of the slots."

It took them about two minutes, while Chris held her gun on McKay. Zippo pushed past him behind the counter and began yanking out drawers, dumping them onto the floor; knives and ladles and silverware clattered in a mad cascade. He pulled out the knobs on the gas range and bent the control shafts at ninety-degree angles. At the counter's end there was a soft-drink dispenser in the shape of a barrel of Hire's Root Beer, on a stand over a set of spigots. The barrel ruptured when it hit the floor, and sticky syrup began to run in rivulets between the planks.

Snake thumbed back the hammer of the .38 and fired six times. From left to right the cooler doors cracked; inside, beer cans exploded in geysers of foam. Shelves toppled, spilling candy bars and canned goods and magazines. A popcorn machine lurched over and shattered, snowing white kernels. Next to it was a carousel hot-dog grill.

Snake picked it up, raised it over his head in a two-handed stance, and tossed it through the front window. Glass splattered around Chris's feet.

McKay came around the counter, but when Chris waved the gun, he stopped. Snake pointed a finger at him. "You won't forget us, McKay. Especially you won't forget the Princess here."

Snake turned to her and said, "Shoot him in the knee."

Chris grinned and shot McKay in the knee.

McKay stumbled back, slapped clumsily at his knee, steadied himself on the counter for a moment with his other hand before going down awkwardly. Pain etched the lines in his face more deeply, and blood dribbled from the ends of his fingers.

"You bastards," he moaned.

"Let's go, Princess," Snake said.

But when he glanced at her as they pulled out of the lot, genuine respect was written on his features.

Inside the Quik-Stop, McKay stood up and wiped his hand on a dish towel, tossing away the gelatin capsule he had palmed. He pulled up the T-shirt and unstrapped a padded girdle, then ripped the mustache from his upper lip, wincing a little as the adhesive plucked at his skin. He laid the windowpane eyeglasses on the counter.

The back door near the end of the counter opened and Vang came in. He was holding a small automatic, and he scanned the room before holstering it. Another man pushed through the door behind him, middle-aged and white-faced. He looked around; fear and anger and outrage marched over his features in that order.

"Get those bastards," he muttered. "You get those bastards, you hear me?"

William Sterling Price was wiping the stage blood from his pants leg. "We plan to, McKay."

A new expression came to McKay's face. "You could have stopped them."

"Maybe," Price said evenly. "But since we were working on a three-minute lead time, it wouldn't have been easy. I'm sorry about your place, but"—Price straightened and his voice cooled—"at least you're still walking on two good legs." Vang was holding the door. "Good luck, McKay."

Vang started the GMC but did not pull out. He looked at Price. "I think our friend Chris is in a lot of danger with those people."

"So do I." Price's voice was a bit weary. "But it doesn't matter what we think, partner. From here we're out of it—and she's on her own."

Chapter Four

The sheriff's deputy was fat: in his dark uniform he looked like an avocado into which someone had jammed four sticks and a toothpick holding a maraschino cherry. He had dewlaps like a bulldog's and an unnatural red blush to his complexion, as if he had been holding his breath for the last three minutes. He wheezed as he came up to where the four of them had pulled over on the shoulder of the two-lane. They were in the high scrub-desert country north of Wells, maybe five miles from the little casino town of Jackpot at the Idaho border.

Chris looked the cop up and down, then turned on her saddle to Snake. "If I was as ugly as this pig, I'd off myself." To the cop: "You must toss your cookies every time you look in the mirror."

"Ease up," Snake said, full of good humor.

"What's your problem, pig?" Chris said to the cop. She shook her head in disgust. "Christ, this slob is panting like a dog. What do you want for Christmas—an iron lung?"

"Be cool, Princess," Snake said. Zippo swung off his bike, turned away, and began to urinate. Crazy George was spooning up a toot of meth from a glass vial. The cop seemed to bother them as much as bad breath.

"What's the problem?" Snake said.

The cop tipped back his Smokey hat and grinned. His slack skin was greasy, as if he were sweating out his own melting fat. "I shot you-all at ninety-six miles per hour, boy."

"You need a new gun," Zippo said, zipping up. "We were going 105 easy."

"Let's see some licenses."

Snake shook his head, as if he felt sorry for the guy. He pulled his chain-drive wallet, dug inside the flap and extracted four bills one at a time, so the cop could see they were one-hundreds.

"Shit," Chris said with genuine disgust.

The cop stared greedily at the money. His eyes were stuck deep in the suet of his face, and spaced too closely together.

Snake held out the cash. "Here you go, pal. Four people, four licenses."

The cop grabbed the money out of Snake's fist. He had fast hands for a fat man.

"Anything else? We got places to go."

The cop fanned the bills like a winning poker hand. "This ought to about do it."

"Then fuck off, pig," Snake said. He jammed down on his kick starter, and gravel sprayed over the cop's feet and legs as they left him standing there counting the money again and smiling a doggish grin. They hit 100 mph before they were out of sight.

Chris watched the road unreel and thought about the Nevada deputy. There were a thousand brave dedicated officers for every bent cop, but the corrupt few did damage out of proportion to their numbers. They were the holes in the fabric of justice through which ruthless hoodlums like the bikers were able to wriggle. The holes began as tiny rips, the kind of low-level bribery she had just seen. But once the cloth was rent, it was easier to widen the tear. The bribes became thousands—or tens of thousands—of dollars. For enough money, you could get away with murder.

Creeps like the fat deputy were only the tip of the iceberg.

The good cops were doing their best to put the rotten

ones out of business. There wasn't anything Chris could do right now to help out on that front—except her damnedest to kick the pins out from under the outlaw biker gangs.

They hit American Falls, on the Snake River in Idaho, late that afternoon. Chris guessed they had come three hundred miles in a little more than three hours. At that rate, a biker with enough guts and stamina—or crystal meth—could make it cross-country in a day and a half. Chris knew that these outlaws had guts enough, or a sort of crazed lack of reasoned fear that amounted to the same thing.

They stopped at a working-class dive on the other side of town, with a couple of pickup trucks and a semi-rig with double sleeper and a stock trailer parked in front. Blinking against the sudden dimness of the place, Chris made out three customers: a guy in a cowboy hat, hunched over a draft beer, and the two truckers, who shut up and turned in unison to stare at the newcomers.

The bartender was a young redheaded guy with the build of a pro wrestler. He wore bib overalls, and from the calluses on his hands, the red sunburn on his neck, and the knots of muscle showing bulging under his shirt, serving drinks was not his regular line. He looked like he could throw a cow over a car one-handed.

"Brew for the crew, dude," Snake said, showing a challenging grin. "Sixer of Coors."

The bartender shook his big head. "We don't need the business."

"What's that mean?"

"We got no use for your kind in this place."

Snake's grin widened. Without taking his eyes from the bartender he said, "Hey, Crazy George—you remember what happened to the last dude who wouldn't sell us beer?"

"Yeah." George's already dilated eyes brightened at the memory. "We fucked hell out of his old lady on the pool table."

"Don't see no old lady around here." Zippo cackled like

56

a moron. "Maybe this dude is queer. Maybe we should fuck hell out of *him*."

"Are you punks looking for trouble?" It was one of the truckers, a big guy in a yellow Budweiser cap.

"Nope," Snake said. "We are looking for a six-pack of suds. Only this dude won't sell it to us." Snake was still staring across the bar at the redheaded guy. "Show some class, Crazy George."

George turned his back on the rest of them and fumbled at his pants. Urine splashed in a thin yellow stream in the center of the coin-op pool table. A widening spot of green felt turned darker.

"You dirty sons of bitches." The trucker came halfway off his stool.

"Over here," Chris said quietly.

The trucker looked at her—and down the paired barrels of the .357 Magnum derringer. He froze for a moment, then barked out a laugh. "Who you figure on shooting, chickie?"

Chris stroked the trigger of the little gun, and behind the trucker a full quart bottle of bourbon exploded. Glass tinkled on the shelf, and amber liquor geysered into the air to rain down in a fine pungent mist. The report of the gun was too loud in the close room.

"I'm figuring on shooting the next asshole who opens his yap," Chris said.

The trucker settled back onto his stool. His eyes were wide and his mouth was open, as if he had just witnessed a levitation.

"Dude," Snake said to the bartender, "I'd say you better get that six-pack. Move smooth—you never know what'll make the Princess here crazy."

The bartender bent to a cooler, straightened with the Coors. Snake made a show of peeling off a twenty-dollar bill from his wad and tossing it on the bar. "Keep the change," he said. "Buy your trucker pal some new pants. He just shit the pair he's got on."

Out front the asphalt was spongy from the day-long heat of the sun. Snake popped a top and swallowed half a can of beer. "You were pretty cool in there, Princess. You are one tough old lady."

"I'm tough," Chris corrected, "but I'm no old lady." She swung onto the saddle of her bike. "Where next, bro?"

"Don't you worry about that, Princess. You'll be there when you get there." He glanced over his shoulder, but the four guys in the bar were holing up until they were sure the demented invaders were well gone.

"I've gone through with the job," Chris protested. "I'm in."

"Not officially. You got to be initiated in front of the whole club."

Behind her, Zippo and Crazy George exchanged high-pitched demented giggles.

"Yes sir," Crazy George rapped. "You gonna like initiation."

"Yeah," Snake said. She'd put him down, and here was a shot back. "You'll like initiation, all right—but not as much as we will."

Chapter Five

Chris Amado had seen some things—but not like this, not ever.

The grassy flat meadow cut by the meander of the Snake River's headwaters was filled with three thousand bikes and four thousand people. The gleaming metal scoots, all raked front wheels and twin pipes and mechanical menace, and the denim-clad rat-haired bearded bikers looked as out of place in this awesome wilderness setting as a rat in a Jell-O mold.

Chris sat her Harley atop the last rise in the dirt road, the motor idling softly. Off to her left, a couple miles away, the great rugged majesty of the three mountains—the Grand, the Middle, and the Petite Teton—towered over them. This was Jackson Hole, the wide grassy swale forty miles south of Yellowstone Park. Down in the town of Jackson, through which they had passed a few minutes earlier, the trade was strictly tourist, with skiing in the winter, and tram rides, wild-west shows, and mimed shoot-outs in the square every high noon during the summer months. The saloons took their decor from western movies, and the souvenir joints did a brisk business in arrowheads from Taiwan, vinyl rattlesnake skins, and Stetson-shaped ashtrays.

But the fecund land north of town was too rich to waste on tourists. This was ranching and farming country, watered by the Snake, fed by the snow-melt runoff from the high mountains stored in Jackson Lake. Richer, more nutritious rangeland did not exist except in some stockman's drunken daydreams.

Snake had finally opened up at the last gas stop, in Swan Valley at the foot of the other side of Teton Pass. Their destination was the annual summer run, hosted by the Outsiders and attended by all the satellite clubs under their control, like a company picnic to reward the loyal workers. This ranch was owned by a onetime Outsider named Gigantic Gene. He'd paid for it with his retirement pension, Snake said without irony.

It must have been some pension, Chris thought, gazing over the place. Her father had been an agricultural expert, and Chris knew she was looking at several *million* dollars' worth of land.

A sheriff's car rolled slowly past them, heading away from this madness. Although it was late afternoon and the hottest part of the day, all the windows of the cruiser were rolled up. Under their tans the deputies' sweating faces were pale and drawn, as if they were explorers who had stumbled upon a prehistoric society of cannibalistic mutants and had barely escaped intact. Snake snapped off an exaggerated salute, and Crazy George flipped them a finger. The cops concentrated on looking straight ahead, like condemned men heading for the rope.

"Come on," Snake said, revving his engine. "Let's scare up Rock."

Snake led them single-file through the encampment, moving at a walk, transmissions geared low and throaty. Eyes turned in their direction: they were Outsiders, and their arrival was ceremonial, a procession. Snake was lieutenant of the master club, second in command of the infrastructure that controlled the actions—and wealth—of the thousands of people present. Anyone wearing Outsider colors—or only riding with them, like Chris—shared the distinction. Cruising through this mass of warped humanity, they were like the retainers in some medieval despot's court, feared and hated and envied by the hoi polloi.

Chris drew as much attention as Snake; she could feel eyes raking over her like the clutching hands of fans grabbing at a celebrity. She threaded her bike through a jumble of parked Harleys and scattered sleeping bags and constantly growing mounds of empty beer cans. In the sixties, Charley Benjamin had told her back at Dennison's, a woman gang member was as rare as a talking dog. Now many gangs were giving a few women full privileges. This wasn't some sudden blossoming of feminist awareness; it was purely expedient. Women could infiltrate where men could not.

But even so, any woman on a bike—especially one as darkly beautiful as Chris, in leathers and braless T-shirt—drew curious stares. Chris was not unaware of the overt eroticism she presented, astride the throbbing deep-voiced silver machine, the incongruous juxtaposition of grace and power, of delicacy and brute force—and most of all of freedom, independence. While a few women were full gang members, the majority remained adjuncts: occasionally as old

60

ladies, more often mamas or simply strange chicks, tolerated for their mindless willingness to suffer, often with apparent pleasure, all manner of sexual abuse. Chris felt the eyes of the women as well, and when she met their gazes she saw vague wistful jealousy, but mostly resignation and acceptance; uncomfortably, Chris thought of whipped puppies.

None of them doubted that Chris was a different story—and so far the satellite-club bikers staring at her were unsure of the plot line. But she was with the Outsiders, and that meant, among other things, hands off. There were no whistles or obscene catcalls, and when she stared down one of the bearded bikers, he usually looked away.

The clubs were forted up in separate camps, their hogs arranged in a loose circle like covered wagons awaiting Indian attack. Most of the gangs had some kind of four-wheeler with them—a van or a pickup truck, usually—to carry the heavier necessities of a run; it was hard to get more than three or four cases of brew on a sled.

Within the circle of bikes, the camp typically consisted of a fire ring in which deadfall branches were piled in anticipation of an after-dark bonfire, and nearby an assortment of coolers filled with ice and beer, or sometimes a keg, iced down in a metal washtub. Strewn around this core were sleeping bags, camp stoves, open bags of chips and beef jerky and other junk food, and mounting piles of garbage: crushed cans, broken wine bottles, candy wrappers, cigarette butts, discarded clothing. The garbage seemed as essential as anything else, as if the bikers could not completely relax without its comforting presence.

Even though the Hole was over a mile above sea level, the July day was hot, and almost everyone had stripped down. One biker wore black boots, a Prussian helmet with a short spear sticking up from the crown, his cutoff, and nothing else. Another had hacked off the legs of his greasy denims below the crotch with his Buck knife; his legs were white as cheese above his black leather boots, the effect more obscene than if he had been naked.

Most of the men tended to be massive and sinewy, as if their muscles recalled earlier days of physical labor. But they also had fat beer guts lopping over their chain belts, pale as whale bellies. Tattoos were so omnipresent they became part of the uniform. Chris saw daggers, death's-heads, nude women in all sorts of impossible contortions. One biker had a foot-wide swastika on his chest, another a giant hand giving the finger. There was "Mother" above a leering spread-legged woman; "Jack the Ripper," "Rape," and "LSD." Some of the insignia were in biker code: "13," representing the thirteenth letter, M for "marijuana"; "DFFL," biker shorthand for "Dope Forever, Forever Loaded"; and most popular, FTW. Here was the essence of the biker creed, the ultimate statement of biker philosophy: "Fuck The World."

No matter how they had stripped down, every biker wore his cutoff, with club colors on the back; a biker's cutoff was like a cowboy's hat, never removed in public, defended to the death. Clubs from all over the country west of the Mississippi were represented, sporting their colors as proudly as a sailor's dress whites. On Chris's left as she putted by were the Satan's Sons, Benjamin's club; to her right, the Badasses. Further on she passed the Crazy Aces, the Wanderers, the Roman Lords, the Widowmakers, the Lethal Lovers, and at least two dozen other outfits. A few of the attendees were independents who occasionally free-lanced when one of the clubs needed an unknown face for an operation; their colors read "Lone Wolf" or "No Club"—or simply "Fuck You."

Many of the women were topless, especially the mamas; a few were naked. One of them turned, and Chris's stomach lurched. The girl could not have been older than seventeen, and she was lithe and small-breasted and still almost pretty. Her skin was tanned and smooth and unmarked—except for the grotesque dark scar on her buttocks, where "Property of the Black Dukes" had been burned into the flesh.

The smell of marijuana was thick as mist, cut by the odors of motor oil and spilled beer and rank human bodies. The women's eyes, and most of the men's, were red-rimmed and unfocused, and at some of the camps Chris spotted big bowls of pills near the beer stash, red Seconals and Nembutal yellow-jackets and pink-heart Dexies. Bikers were nibbling at them like salted peanuts, washing them down with swigs of beer in dosages that would be lethal to anyone but an inured doper.

Some of the men had gone to a lot of trouble to dude up for the occasion. One Widowmaker had shaved his head except for a Mohawk skunk stripe, which he had dyed purple, along with his beard. Several of the Satan's Sons, the Tucson club, wore beaded Apache headbands or matched pairs of thick silver bracelets studded with chunks of turquoise. A huge Thrillkiller with a flat porcine face wore a brass ring through the septum of his nose; several others wore heavy gold jewelry in pierced earlobes. A glazed-eyed biker in cutoff and nothing else had a big X-shaped scar on his chest, each leg a foot long; it was knifework, too precise to have been done accidentally. Chris felt vaguely nauseated—but maybe it was just the smell.

"We gonna have us a time, Princess," Zippo said over his shoulder. "I bet you can't hardly wait."

But Chris was staring off to her left, to an encampment on the edge of the vast sea of outlaws. "What the hell . . ." she said involuntarily.

Zippo dropped back beside her. "Them are the Manic Mamas." He grinned. "One mean set of woofies," he added with admiration.

The Manic Mamas looked like a twisted vision from a leather freak's most perverse wet dream: all sleek black jumpsuits over push-up bras, bouffant hairdos, and sullen challenging expressions. The club name was ironic: none of these ladies was anybody's mama. There were a dozen of them, chugging down beer, watching the grand entrance of

Snake's group with malevolent resignation. A couple were sitting on their bikes; as they revved the motors, their sleepy eyes widened, as if they could absorb horsepower between their leather-clad legs.

"The Mamas run the street whores in Denver," Zippo said. "When they came into the Outsider nation, we tried using them when we needed a chick to get inside someplace for us, but it didn't work out. Them Mamas are meaner than half the bros in this place—every time a citizen tried to lay a hand on one of them, he was sucking at a razor slash."

Ahead of them, Crazy George's hog whined, and his sled reared up on the back wheel and veered toward the Mamas' campsite. None of them moved. At the last moment George slewed the bike around and came to a stop, the front tire dropping and bouncing on the ground, a foot from one of the Mama's cycles. Crazy George cackled. The Mamas looked at him as if he were vermin.

"Let's take care of business, George," Snake called. "Then we party hearty." He goosed his bike past the leather-clad women.

The Outsiders' own camp was on the far side up a small rise, a position of honor from which they could survey the entire site. Chris recognized most of the bikers from the barroom in Barstow. They were slugging down brew and wine and pills as madly as everyone else—except for the good-looking blond surfer-boy who had given her such a penetrating look when she walked into the Hellhole. He was staring at her the same way now. His little ferret-faced buddy stood close by, blank-faced, as if unsure how he had gotten here.

Chris cranked at the accelerator and her scoot leaped up next to Snake. "Who are those guys?"

Snake followed her gesture, then laughed. "That's Pretty Boy and Rat."

"Rat?" Chris echoed incredulously. She laughed.

"Yeah, those bros are pretty close, if you know what I mean—but that don't make them cream puffs." Snake frowned.

"Rat, he's not so smart, but Pretty Boy . . . he's, you know, *weird*."

"You mean 'queer.' ' '

Snake shrugged, as if he'd lost interest.

The ranch house was set back from the river on top of the little rise they were climbing, a neat log building fronted by a canopied front porch with some cane lawn furniture, set amid a stand of Lombardy poplars planted decades earlier. Gigantic Gene rose from a chair to greet them.

The onetime Outsider was in his fifties. He stood several inches over six feet and could not have weighed less than five hundred pounds. His body was a sphere; in coveralls he looked like a denim balloon. He wore lace-up boots big as skillets; his hands were the size of baseball mitts, his fingers like bratwursts. His big head was upholstered in gray beard and long full gray hair. His eyes were incongruously small, porcine and sunk deep into his bloated face.

Crazy George leaped from his bike, flew up the two stairs to the porch, and planted a biker kiss on Gigantic Gene's lips. In Gene's arms, the scrawny speed freak looked like a child.

A petite, pleasant-looking woman, neatly dressed in a gingham dress, stepped out onto the porch behind them. Her gray-streaked hair was done up in a bun held in a snood, and she was dusting flour from her hands. She smiled at the bikers like a mother welcoming her son's college buddies arriving for a home-cooked meal.

"You know the bros, Gene." Snake swung off his scoot. "Meet the Princess."

"How do." Gigantic Gene had a voice as deep as an artesian well. "This here is Wee Winnie, my old lady."

The petite woman nodded and murmured a greeting. Chris kicked down the Harley's stand and followed Snake inside.

The cabin's shades were drawn, so it took Chris's eyes several seconds to adjust. In one shadowed corner, Rock straddled a kitchen chair turned backward. His hog-leg Colt hung over his thigh, and he held a cup of coffee. He turned his black sunglasses in Chris's direction. This was his temporary domain by virtue of his office, and he was as at home in it as a king in his throne room. His consort stood behind him; Lizzie's eyes burned in the dimness as she stared at Chris.

Rock listened without interrupting as Snake reported on the job they had done on McKay in Ely. Rock's expression was impassive as a statue's, and when Snake was finished, Rock stared silently at him for a good half-minute. "Okay," he said finally. "You bros earned some partying."

George and Zippo did not have to be told twice. Sunlight chased the dimness as they darted out the door like campers getting off the bus at Disneyland. Snake hesitated, then followed. Gene and Winnie had remained discreetly out on the porch; as an ex-Outsider Gene had status, but he was no longer privy to gang business, as much for his own protection as for club security.

"You too, Liz," Rock said, watching Chris. "The Princess and I got to have a private talk."

"I bet you do."

Rock sighed. "Get some fresh air, Lizzie."

Lizzie stared over Rock at Chris, her hard face mottled with anger.

"I'll leave a little for you," Chris said nastily. "After I'm done."

"That's enough," Rock said. "Move, Lizzie."

"I will like hell."

Rock turned in his chair and pointed a finger up at her. Lizzie gasped. She stepped back from the chair, sidled away. She shot a vicious glare at Chris as she went out. Sooner or later, this was going to break out into real trouble—which was fine with Chris.

Rock folded his arms on the back of the chair. "What do you want with the Outsiders, Princess?" he asked thoughtfully.

"I told you."

Rock shook his head, as if genuinely perplexed. "Okay, so you're clean so far. You've handled yourself, you haven't missed a step, and you haven't slipped. Shooting McKay took guts. There's only the one thing."

"Which is?"

"I got a bad hunch about you, Princess." Rock grinned almost apologetically. "And as a general rule I go with my hunch—which is to throw your ass out of here."

"Suit yourself." Chris turned to the door. "I'll give Apeman a big kiss for you."

Rock said nothing, but Chris did not move, waiting him out. "You take some chances, Princess," he said finally.

"Yeah. I'm that way sometimes."

"I don't know who or what you are—but if I ever get the idea you were spying for Apeman and the Mad Dogs, you're dead. Not quick, and not without a shitload of pain."

"I'm what I said: a chick on the run looking for a club. I've found one, and I've done what I was supposed to, and by the rules—if they mean anything, bro—I should be in.

"I'm not stupid," Chris went on, "I keep my ears open. I know some things. One is that Apeman wants to bury you and take over your turf. Well, between you and me, bro, I think Apeman is a scumbag. That's why I want to throw in with the Outsiders. But if you won't play ball, I'm betting Apeman will. I've been around, Rock: I know I've got one friend in the world, and that's me."

For a long time Rock stared back impassively. Then he nodded and took a sip of coffee. "Get yourself a brew, Princess—you earned it."

"Fine," Chris said coolly.

But outside on the porch she allowed herself a sigh of relief. The hardest part was over: she was in; she was an Outsider.

Which did not mean this day had come to a peaceful conclusion. Lizzie stood at the foot of the porch steps, and when Chris ignored her and tried to push past, the big-breasted blond grabbed her arm above the elbow, surprisingly strong fingers digging into Chris's bicep.

"You keep your hands off my man, bitch," Lizzie hissed.

"Get fucked." Chris spoke loud enough to draw the attention of Crazy George and Zippo and a few others. They drew closer, attracted to the possibility of a cat fight like flies to a Popsicle.

"You think you're something," Lizzie said. "What you are is a cunt."

Chris planted a hand on Lizzie's chest and shoved hard, and the other woman, taken by surprise, let go of Chris's arm and sat down hard in the dirt. The other bikers pressed closer. Lizzie gathered her feet under her.

"Hold it!"

Rock came down the porch steps and stared at Lizzie. "That's enough."

Lizzie got her feet under her—and lurched at Chris.

Rock caught her wrist and whipped her around. His free hand shot out in a vicious slap, forehand and then backhand, magically quick. Blood dribbled from the corner of Lizzie's mouth.

For maybe five seconds nobody moved.

Then Chris Amado laughed in Lizzie's bloody face, before turning on her heel and showing her back to all of them.

Chapter Six

Someone had taken trouble in building the bonfire. Thick cottonwood branches were tepeed in a cone, with brush piled in the middle. There was a small flat bench of land here, ending in a cutbank that dropped to the sluggish river ten feet below. Across the flat on the other side, the Tetons speared into the star-chased night sky.

From the main encampment, a couple of hundred yards across the field, came the sounds of outlaw party fun: lupine howls of pleasure or anger, the screams of women, all of it underlain by the constant ambient growl of Harley mills. But as drunk or stoned as they were, no member of any satellite club intruded on the small gathering near the river. This was an occasion of great solemnity, limited to Outsiders; no outlaw biker would violate the sanctity of an initiation ceremony.

Chris Amado stood a little to one side, smoking a cigarette. The rest of the club ignored her. She was not sure what was about to happen, but she did not expect it to be pleasant. The idea was to stay cool and show class, whatever these animals dished out.

During the evening she'd met most of the other Outsiders, and learned something about hierarchy. Rock had been president for several years, but Snake had moved up to the vice-presidency only a few months before, when his predecessor, a biker named Gutbucket, was busted. "An undercover pig popped him in a bar in Oakland," Snake told her. "Got him on a concealed weapon for a razor he was toting, and then slapped on a dope bust 'cause he had a vial of crank. Chickenshit crap." The cops didn't usually bother with that kind of pettiness, Snake went on; some of the Outsiders suspected it was a frame—set up by the Mad Dogs.

Crazy George opened to her too. Like all speed freaks, he loved to rap; the trick was in keeping his train of thought from jumping the tracks. Snake was skating on glass, he told her; there was tension between him and Rock. Gutbucket had been a popular vice-president, and Snake, knowing that Gutbucket would be trying to regain his office when he finished his downtime, was acting maybe a little too ambitious in solidifying his own hold.

Crazy George was road captain, in charge of run logistics. The sergeant-at-arms, a biker named Bear, was wandering around the cone of bonfire wood as if impatient to see flames. He wore a calf-length fur coat that would have been rejected at a thrift shop: patches of fur were missing, and what was left had a permanent case of mange. Despite the summer heat, Bear apparently kept the coat on at all times, and there was a perpetual veneer of sweat on his face; an odor of equal parts of body stink and mildewed fur swirled around him like a private atmosphere.

The Outsider who looked most out of place was called Blinker. He was a little older than the others, close to forty by Chris's guess, a slight, narrow-shouldered man with almost delicate hands and quick nervous gestures. His face was clean-shaven and his hairline had receded to the crown of his head; he wore thick rimless glasses that glimmered in the starlight. Blinker was club treasurer, overseer of the Outsiders' entire financial empire. The satellite clubs hired accountants and tax advisers locally, but it was Blinker who coordinated their efforts. He had been a CPA with a national accounting firm until he was caught juggling a client's ledger books in a complex conspiracy involving fraud, embezzlement, and a corporate takeover. Since he was a white-collar crook with no record, all but two years of his sentence was suspended, but his career was over—until he met a couple of Thrillkillers in the joint. Six months after going to work for the satellite club, Blinker was called up to the Outsiders, and six months after that he was treasurer; a dude who could rewrite the books of a Fortune 500 company was someone the Outsiders could admire and respect.

Another dozen Outsiders made up the initiation party, along with Gigantic Gene, invited as a courtesy. Pretty Boy stood off to the side as usual with his little bro Rat. He tossed his tousled blond hair and made a show of turning away when Chris looked in his direction, and she wondered vaguely what was eating the guy. She hadn't even spoken with him. Lizzie was missing—Chris had not seen her since the confrontation at the ranch house—and so was Snake. Rock was off near the edge of the bench, talking in a low voice with Crazy George; the crankster biker's head was bobbing in a continuous nod of agreement with whatever Rock was telling him. Most of the rest were drinking from cans of beer, but there was none of the raucous behavior that characterized the rest of the encampment. This was a genuinely solemn occasion for these hooligans, Chris realized with some surprise. The term they used to refer to each other—"bro"—was significant; the brotherhood that came with being a biker, perverted as it was, was of paramount importance. As much as they disdained any notions of sentimentality or society, belonging meant something to these people. They were outcasts, screw-ups, and sociopaths—and they could find society only in the company of their own kind.

Around the waiting bonfire there was a stir. Bear produced a jerrican of gasoline from somewhere and doused the pyramided branches, then lit a full book of matches and tossed it. Smoky flames lashed the darkness immediately, throwing eerie shadows on the gathered bikers. Every eye was on Chris.

Snake appeared in the glow of the light, carrying a folded square of denim. He shook it out, and Chris saw it was a cutoff with Outsider colors stitched to the back. The denim was new and unfaded, and the shoulder seam where the sleeves had been hacked off hadn't begun to ravel. Rock moved up beside Snake and took the jacket, looked it over and nodded his approval. The other Outsiders pulled closer behind him, their faces reddish in the fire's glow, their expressions taut with anticipation.

Rock held out the colors so Chris could see the death's-head and the crossed revolvers, the legend "Outsiders MC." "These colors declare that you are an Outsider," Rock said. "No one takes your colors. If someone bad-mouths your colors, you stomp him. Anyone else who wears these colors is your bro, and a bro is always right. Anyone pulls any shit on a bro, and every other bro comes to his aid. One bro stomps a dude, everyone joins in."

Rock spread the cutoff on the grass, colors up. He straightened and pulled his Buck knife, unfolded the blade. "Come here, Princess."

Chris faced him across the colors. No one spoke. Chris put out her hand, palm up.

Rock gripped her wrist roughly and drew the razor-sharp point of the knife from one side of her palm to the other. Chris clenched her jaw and kept her face neutral. Rock wielded the knife with surgical deftness; the cut welled a bit of blood, but it was no deeper than a scratch.

Chris lowered her hand and let the blood run off her fingertips onto the colors.

"All right," Rock announced. Chris stepped back and the other bros surged forward. They did not bother to line up, just got a hand or foot in as best they could. Boot heels ground the jacket into the dirt; beer splashed over the colors; spittle flew.

Bear was standing a little apart, not participating. But when the knot of bikers was finished, he came forward. He turned his back to Chris, and a moment later his urine splattered over the now-filthy colors.

Bear stepped back and joined the others. It was Chris's move now. The others stared at her with rabid anticipation.

Chris picked up the reeking jacket by the collar. Someone giggled. Chris looked from one biker to the next, meeting each stare in turn.

She threw the cutoff over her shoulders and pulled it on.

"Aw right," Crazy George muttered.

Chris stood arms akimbo and grinned wickedly. "Who do you have to screw around here to get a beer?"

For a moment no one moved. She had performed to their satisfaction so far, but the question still hung in the air: could this chick show real class?

Bear stepped out of the crowd and handed her a full can. Chris popped the top and took a big swig—

—and spewed it back in Bear's face.

For a perilous hanging moment they stood like that, Chris's arrogant stance daring Bear to object, the beer dripping from his sopping beard.

Then Chris whooped with laughter and upended the rest of the can over her own head. "Let's party hearty, bros." She grabbed another beer out of someone's hand, shaking it before opening it, so froth sprayed over the knot of them. That broke up any solemnity left. Bikers charged the beer coolers.

Chris followed on their heels. Rock was standing off to himself, watching her thoughtfully through the black lenses that hid his eyes. The hell with him, Chris thought. She had pulled it off; she was in now.

She had taken every serving of crap he'd dished out. Pretty soon now it was going to come flying back in his face.

Chapter Seven

"Gotta tap a kidney," Chris slurred. "Gotta go show off the Outsider colors." Crazy George was standing beside her, staring dementedly into the flames. Chris lurched off, stopping at the cooler. "A brew for the road," she announced. "Gonna show class and kick ass." Rock looked at her and said nothing; he was the only one not drinking. "See ya 'round, bro," Chris said saucily, and staggered into the darkness.

She tripped over a tree root and almost fell. "Son of a bitch," she said, and giggled. She set a course for the main encampment and weaved toward it.

When she was certain she was out of sight of the Outsiders, Chris straightened. She opened the can of beer and poured half of it out, then moved on normally.

They had been celebrating her initiation for several hours now, and although it had to be two in the morning, there was no sign the party was letting up. She was careful to demonstrate that she could gargle down the beer and hit the downers as hard as any bro—except that the palmed pills went into her pocket, and most of the suds soaked into the dirt while she was supposedly off taking care of business.

If the gigantic biker bivouac had been a bizarre scene when she arrived, a full day of hard drinking and doping had pushed it beyond weirdness. The encampment looked like the hell vision of a schizophrenic on bad LSD. Chris passed a biker sitting on his scoot, kick stand down but the motor on; the biker was cranking the accelerator, and each time the engine whined his eyes brightened, as if he were wired to the alternator.

At the next camp, a scooter tramp had passed out, and a crowd of his brothers was gathered around. Chris wandered closer, and one of the bikers started to say, "Hey, woofie, come on in . . ." But then he saw her colors, and his slack expression glimmered momentary sobriety. "Sorry, bro. Have a suds on the Crazy Horsemen."

"Why not?" Chris took the proffered can. One of the Horsemen was twisting a length of ignition wire around his unconscious bro's ankles, and another was doing up his wrists. When he was trussed up satisfactorily, the guy who'd come on to Chris said, "Do him, bros."

Books of matches flared around the circle—and landed in the crashed biker's lap.

The guy snuffled in his sleep and his nostrils flared. Suddenly his eyes flew open like window shades. He sat half up, stared at the flaming matchbooks in the crotch of his denims. He tried to roll over, but he was too drunk to coordinate the movement.

"Piss on me!" the guy screamed. "For God's sake, someone piss on me."

Chris pushed between two of the Aces and poured a stream of beer in the guy's lap. The fire hissed out. An acrid smell cut the smoke; the guy had wet his own pants. His bros began to laugh.

"Thanks for the suds," Chris said, and got away from there.

A naked fat woman came running down the alley between camps; she was laughing, and her pendulous breasts and the flab of her stomach flopped with each step. She shot past Chris, and a moment later a Harley tore after her. The guy riding it was naked too. At the next camp, two bikers were standing by their fire talking quietly. As Chris passed, one of them turned slightly and started urinating into the flames. "If you ain't a biker," he said solemnly to his bro, "you ain't shit."

Chris had seen enough—enough to turn her stomach. Besides, she did not want Rock getting too curious about where she was. She turned back toward the initiation party. It was the last place she wanted to be—between clean sheets was the first—but she was a biker now, a bro, and she remembered what Charley Benjamin had said, what Dennison had drilled into her: you did not play the role, you lived it—or you died.

Someone grabbed her roughly by the arm and pulled her around. He was about her height and slightly built, and he wore the smirk that some small men adapt as compensation, a bullying coward's challenge to all comers.

"Where'd you get the colors, suckie?" The guy stank of stale beer. His own cutoff read "No Club." "You rip off one of the bros while he was passed?"

"You got about one second to let go of my arm," Chris said.

"And after that?"

"After that, I'm going to kick your face in." As she said it, Chris realized it would be a pleasure. This had not been an easy night, and this stinking pig richly deserved to get his teeth handed to him in a baggie.

But before Chris could slam an elbow into the middle of the loner's leering mug, someone behind her said, "What goes on, bro?"

Chris stepped back from the loner. Two Manic Mamas were flanking her, their black leather jumpsuits gleaming in the firelight. The one to Chris's left was a hawk-faced blond; the other had dark Latino features. *"Que pasa, hermano?"* she murmured.

"Nada." Chris laughed. *"El puerco,"* she added, nodding at the grinning pint-sized loner.

"Hey, hey," the guy cut in. "I always did go for the dark meat." He stepped forward and gave the Latino Mama a serving of his smirk.

Then he reached out and squeezed her breast, deliberately, roughly. "I always say, a woman's a lot like a bike," he drawled. "Just 'cause she's fast and cheap don't mean she's any good."

Chris had time to step back and think: *Jesus, what a moron.* Then the blond Mama's hand flashed and the loner screamed and stopped grinning. He slapped at his cheek and blood oozed between his fingers. He lowered the hand, stared at the gore. The cut started at his earlobe and ended at the corner of his mouth, the skin peeled back like the split in an overripe tomato.

The blond Mama wiped the razor clean on the guy's arm.

"You cunt," the loner whined.

The Latino Mama punched him in the face. He grunted and went down, and the Latino was on top of him and sitting on his chest, her knees pinning his arms. The guy shook his head groggily; blood drooled down his face.

The blond Mama crouched and drew the razor along the inseam of the guy's denims, parting the cloth like paper. The loner wore no underwear. He was coming around now, trying to sit up. The Latino punched him again, not hard enough to knock him out, and he stopped struggling. His genitals were small and shriveled with his pain and fear.

The blond Mama lifted his cock and held the knife to its base. She looked up at Chris and grinned. "Want a souvenir?"

Chris returned the smile. "I don't want nothing this dude's got—but thanks for the help."

The loner was mewling like a kitten. "Please, Jesus God, please." He began to sob.

"Always glad to back a bro," the blond Mama said.

"Buenas noches," the Latino added.

Chris had gone a half-dozen steps when the loner biker screamed. The sound was high-pitched and keening and full of terror, the noise an animal makes because it has not previously experienced true pain. It rose and fell for maybe ten seconds and then stopped abruptly, but for a long time after, Chris still heard it in her mind.

From the shadows on the edge of the bench where the initiation had gone down, Chris could see the Outsiders were still partying at the same manic pace. She took a breath of night air, concentrating on making her drunken stagger look good.

"Hey there, Princess," a voice said softly.

It was the blond biker and his boy companion—Pretty Boy and Rat, she remembered.

"What's happenin', bro?" Chris slurred.

"You and me, babe," Pretty Boy said. "That's what's happening."

His little buddy wet his lips with his tongue. "Listen, Pretty Boy, why don't we—?"

"Fetch yourself some brew, Rat."

The little guy hesitated, then scampered off toward the fire. Chris started in the same direction.

"Wait up." He did not touch her, but she stopped anyway.

"I'm waitin'."

"How 'bout it, babe?"

Wonderful, Chris thought. Tonight they were coming out of the woodwork. "How 'bout what?"

"You and me."

"I don't like to be rushed, except on a scoot." She smiled and started toward the fire.

Pretty Boy stepped in front of her.

"Look," Chris said patiently, "I thought . . ." She inclined her head toward Rat, who was hovering off to the side, sipping nervously at a beer.

"Don't be jumping to conclusions, babe."

She'd had enough. "Don't be calling me 'babe.' "

Pretty Boy smiled, almost sadly. "Look, Princess, you are a bro now, sure. Nobody is gonna jump on you—'specially no fellow Outsider bro, like me. But that don't change it."

"Change what, bro?" She put a sarcastic twist on the last word.

"We're gonna make it, you and me—sooner or later, whether you want it or not. You're gonna beg for it."

Chris smiled and leaned a little closer. "Fuck you, bro," she said in a low voice.

She turned and headed into the light of the bonfire, careful to walk a bit unsteadily. Then she saw Rock, standing by himself near the edge of the clearing, sipping from his cup, staring at her. Chris wondered how long he'd been listening, but his expression revealed nothing. He nodded as she weaved past, and she said, "Hey there, bro," and didn't stop. The hell with it, she decided. She'd dealt with enough for one night; if Pretty Boy wanted trouble, he'd have to wait his turn.

Chapter Eight

The kid was about twenty, with clean open features and dark tousled hair that made him look vaguely like a Kennedy. He wore a yellow nylon windbreaker over a blue Williams College T-shirt, cotton twill slacks, and Nike jogging shoes. His girl had pixie-cut blond hair, and the last vestiges of her baby fat filled her designer jeans. She stared at the crowd of bikers surrounding her, alternately horrified and fascinated, like a researcher who has succeeded in breeding a two-headed dog.

"I'm as patriotic as the next guy," the kid said earnestly. "But sometimes you've got to face up to facts. This is a hell of a bike."

He swept one hand around palm up, like Ed Sullivan bringing on Topo Gigio. The bike was a big cherry-red Kawasaki GPz1100 that might have been new that morning. The double overhead-cam four-cylinder engine was clean enough to fry eggs on, and the black-enamel dual pipes were as perfect as modern art. Excess stipple rubber extruded during injection molding stuck out from the sides of the deep-tread Dunlop tires.

"I'm not putting down the Harley," the kid said generously. "They were damned good bikes in their day. But we are talking zero to sixty in four-point-two. We are talking an eleven-point-twenty-two standing quarter-mile, we are talking fifty-seven miles per hour at ninety-five hundred rpm—*in first gear.*'' The kid reeled off the numbers like a sports fanatic listing the home team's stats.

He had come down the dirt road into the encampment a few minutes earlier, the chubby blond girl clinging tightly to his waist. The Satan's Sons camp circle was the first one at that edge of the ranch, so he pulled to a careful stop there. ''How you guys doing?'' A couple of the Sons glanced in the kid's direction, and one bro burped. ''I met some sheriff's deputies along the road, and the way they talked, you guys were supposed to be pretty dangerous.'' The kid chuckled, as if that were a fine joke for them all to share. ''I told them we cyclists stuck together.''

''Cyclist?'' one of the Sons echoed. ''What the fuck is a *cyclist*?'' The blond girl licked her lips and leaned forward to whisper in the kid's ear, and the kid shook his head impatiently.

''Digital fuel injection,'' the kid was saying now. He'd finally drawn a couple of beer-can-toting Sons over to his Kawasaki. ''Five-speed transmission, shaft drive, electric starter, 9.5mm valve lift.'' He was on a roll, like a life-insurance salesman who'd gotten a widow's ear.

As club president, Rodger the Dodger had been hanging back near the keg; it would not be cool to show interest too quickly in some punk wannabee like this kid. Now he drew a fresh glass of suds and hauled his three hundred pounds over to the little knot of Sons around the bike. He had been on crank and brew and no sleep since the run had begun twenty-four hours earlier; his eyes were red as whorehouse lamps, his ratty hair and beard stiff with dried stale beer.

The rest of the Sons pulled back to make way. *''Bueno,''* Pancho Rauncho murmured, as if Rodger's appearance signaled the beginning of the real fun. Footlong, the Sons' vice-president, licked his lips, his eyes darting from Rodger to the girl. They hadn't had a fresh young suckie pull the train for the whole club for weeks, not since that Mex bitch they'd turned out after the Fourth of July coyote run.

The blond girl shrank back a bit as Rodger the Dodger circled the bike, sipping at his beer and nodding judiciously, as if he were judging zucchini at the county fair. The clean-cut kid watched expectantly. Finally Rodger looked at him for the first time.

"Fuckin' Jap shit," Rodger rumbled.

The kid's jaw dropped like he'd been gut-shot. "Hey, man, this is one hell of—"

"What's this pig weigh?" Rodger cut in. "About a half-ton probably, huh?"

The kid shrugged. "Not quite."

Rodger the Dodger pinked one of the dual chrome mirrors with a forefinger. "Look at this garbage, buncha extra-weight crap. Why'n't ya get a stereo and a CB, kid? Fuckin' bike probably steers like a Peterbilt."

The kid drew himself up and squared his shoulders. "It'll beat your Harley," he said stoutly, like a loyal soldier volunteering for a suicide mission.

Maybe he was. Chris Amado stood off to the side and pretended to sip from a can of Satan's Sons' beer. She had been prowling the run-grounds, picking up whatever intelligence she could about the various gangs. The Outsider colors on her cutoff made her a welcome guest at any club's fort-up. But there was nothing she could do about the scene shaping up here, not without unraveling everything she had accomplished so far.

Rodger the Dodger's stiff red beard parted in a big grin, showing teeth as dark as roots. The other Sons gathered around, smelling action like a dog smells fear.

"That rise there, top of the dirt road." Rodger the Dodger pointed a thick finger at the spot where the kid had first appeared, maybe a half-mile away. "You think you can stay on that Jap bike for that far?"

The kid tried another grin, but it did not sit easy on his

face. This was working out not at all as he'd pictured. The girl touched at his arm and said, "Maybe we ought to go, Jimmy."

"*Si, cabrón.*" Pancho Rauncho said. "Maybe you run away, you chickenshit gringo son-bitch."

The kid did not want to look bad in front of the girl. "Just a friendly race, right?" he asked Rodger hopefully.

"Oh, sure, sure. Only let's put a couple bucks on it, just to make it interesting."

That was more like it. The kid nodded. "Say ten dollars?"

"Say one hundred dollars."

The kid gulped. "All right."

"Put it up," Rodger the Dodger ordered.

"That's all right." The kid smiled. "It's a gentleman's bet."

"I ain't never had a gentleman's bet with a Kawasaki guy in my life. Put up the fuckin' cash—your suckie can hold it." Rodger the Dodger showed the girl his brown teeth. "You ain't gonna run off with the bucks, are you, honeybuns?"

"No sir," the girl said. Several of the Sons guffawed.

"I'll keep an eye on her," Footlong said. He pulled her off to the side by the elbow, not gently.

"What else you gonna keep on her, Footlong?" Scuz called.

"Whatever, I got firsts."

"You always got firsts, bro."

"I just loosen 'em up for you dudes," Footlong drawled.

The girl stared up at him for a moment, then shook her head very slightly, as if she had decided to believe this had nothing to do with her.

Rodger the Dodger's bike was a radical gooseneck; the wheelbase was double stock, so the front forks were as long as the rest of the bike put together. The power plant was a 74-cubic-inch early shovelhead, and the only decoration was a stylized nude on the Sportster tank. The bike was built for speed—but so was the kid's Kawasaki. In a fair head-to-head showdown this was anyone's scoot race.

The kid flicked the ignition key and the GPz1100 coughed discreetly to life. Rodger grinned and brought his huge bulk down on the hog's kick starter, cranking the feed so the engine bellowed out a challenging roar. "You ready, kid?" The college guy nodded, a little whitely. As almost an afterthought, he reached around to the rack, unstrapped his helmet, and pulled it on. Someone snickered, and the kid reddened.

From somewhere a skinny dark-haired chick appeared, one of the Sons' mamas. She took up a position between the bikes and a little in front of them, stripped her T-shirt off over her head, and waved it in a slow circle. Her small breasts jiggled in synchronization.

Rodger nodded, and the mama whipped down the T-shirt like a green flag.

The kid got the jump, but that was no surprise. Everyone knew the Kawasaki was quicker off the line. Everyone also knew that Rodger the Dodger, for all his huge beer gut and manic grin, was as skilled a scooter tramp as anyone who ever rode, graceful as a gymnast when on his hog. He was gambling that the biker, not the bike, would win this run.

It looked like a good bet when the kid lost momentary control, his front tire swerving in the dirt before he wrestled the heavy handlebars straight again. But he'd lost speed in the maneuver, enough so Rodger the Dodger could pull up alongside.

That's when the good bet turned into a sure thing.

At fifty miles an hour and accelerating over the rough hard-packed dirt, Rodger the Dodger's foot shot out and kicked at the Kawasaki's front wheel.

The Kawasaki wavered on the edge of dumping, but then the kid had control again. He looked over at Rodger, his eyes wide with astonishment. Rodger laughed in the wind and gunned his hog.

A hard-set look of determination gripped the kid's face. Dammit, he was riding the faster bike, and he could still beat the Harley to the rise, two hundred yards distant now.

As the kid pulled even with the Harley again, Rodger the Dodger leaned over, grabbed the edge of the Kawasaki's fairing, and yanked with all his strength.

The kid's scream was audible above the engines' roar.

The Kawasaki shot off the shoulder of the dirt road. The front tire hit the barrow pit and the bike jackknifed, catapulting the kid into the air in one direction, the bike flipping end over end in another. The machine hit with a whine of wrenching metal, and the engine belched wretchedly before coughing to a stop.

Rodger the Dodger continued to the top of the rise. He stood on his pegs and raised a clenched fist in victory, then rode leisurely back to where the kid had dumped. The helmet had probably saved his life, or at least his head—the rest of him wasn't in such good shape. His left arm was twisted around at a contorted angle. It was slick with blood, and a sliver of bone showed whitely through the bicep. A few yards away, his new Kawasaki was a pile of junk. The kid stared at it, then up at Rodger the Dodger, and shook his head, in pain and shock and denial.

Below, the chubby blond girl began to scream. There was the sharp crack of a slap, and the scream stopped. Rodger the Dodger grinned down at the kid, then rode back to the starting line. Footlong had one of the girl's arms bent up behind her, but he let go as Rodger dismounted.

"To the victor go the spoils," Rodger said.

The girl held out a trembling fistful of dollars. Rodger grabbed the money in one hand, a can of beer in the other. He swilled down half the brew, then grabbed the girl and planted an ugly wet kiss on her mouth, his hand kneading viciously at her breast. When he was done he grinned at Footlong. "For once you get seconds, bro."

The girl began to scream again. This time they let her.

On the hill, the kid had managed to climb to his feet. He stared for a moment, cradling his shattered arm close to his body. But there was nothing he could do for the girl now. He turned and trudged over the rise, trailing drops of blood, putting his back to this sudden impossible nightmare violation of all that was decent and real.

Chris said, "Thanks for the brew, bros," and got out of there. The chubby bond girl was whimpering now, and suddenly Chris wanted desperately to be somewhere where she could not hear the pathetic sound. The mission was everything, she told herself; if the outlaw alliance were not stopped and the gangs broken, hundreds, even thousands of people would suffer much worse than a pair of kids without the sense to take their hands out of a fire. The bikers would go on shooting the McKays of the world in the knee, or killing them outright, would continue to push their drugs and protection and kick around anyone who got in their way, for the sake of money and the heady perverse sadistic thrill of it. Chris told herself all this and went on walking.

But while she could still hear them, the girl's moans traced an icy finger down the ridge of her spine.

It was approaching twilight, and the partying had been going on continuously for over thirty hours. The essential brutishness of the biker was innate: forted up with other bikers and without citizens to abuse, he abused himself. A large percentage of the profits generated by the outlaws' illegal enterprises went into drugs. Since the sixties, bikers had been heavy users of sedatives like Seconal, Amytal, and Nembutal, although the soporifics had little calming effect on their aggressiveness. But now they could afford even stronger and more lethal narcotics, which they embraced with typical manic single-mindedness. Amphetamines in their various forms, from pink-heart Dexedrines to back-street-lab "whites" and even pure crystal, were everywhere; the manufacture and distribution of "crank" had been the bikers' first serious foray into organized crime. At several camps, in parody of the dilettante's silver spoon, Chris saw silver bowls of cocaine; there had to be several dozen pounds of the stuff on the ranch; at street prices, that much coke would be worth a couple of million dollars, paid for at the expense of the citizens the bikers walked all over.

The Outsider colors on Chris's back, somewhat cleaner now thanks to an early-morning dip in the Snake, continued to draw attention, respect, and invitations to share a beer, a slug of wine, a snort, anything she wanted. A friendly grin and any halfway coherent demurral was enough to keep her moving; by now most of the outlaws on this run had reached their destination: mindless oblivion on as much beer and dope as a human body could absorb without shutting down completely.

One zombie-eyed biker stalked past Chris, stiff as Frankenstein's monster. He walked to the edge of the cutbank over the river and kept walking; a half-second after he disappeared, Chris heard the splash. It was probably the first time he'd been fully immersed since baptism. Two bikers were urinating on a bro who had crashed, mindless as mongrels. At the next camp an outlaw was playing horsey astride a fat naked mama crouched on all fours, whipping at her buttocks with his wallet chain while his bros cheered lethargically. The blond Manic Mama who'd been so quick with the razor the previous night was passed out in the cold ashes of a fire ring, her black leathers smeared with gray and torn down the front.

Chris moved through the filth and degradation, forcing a smile here, a friendly nod there. She was careful not to hurry; she was just an Outsider, making the rounds at sunset to see that everyone was partying hearty. But her drifting course was taking her along a circular route to the ranch house—because there, in the front room, it was beginning to come down. Rock was holding council with the Outsider officers and the presidents of the major satellite clubs. The topic was Apeman and the Mad Dogs, and what to do about them.

Chris had to know what they planned, and quick—if she

wanted the chance to make certain that the two biker clubs clashed head to head.

The sun was behind the Tetons by now, and full dark was maybe twenty minutes away. Gigantic Gene and Wee Winnie were drinking wine with Lizzie and a couple of Crazy Horsemen near the edge of the encampment. Chris nodded and flashed a thumbs-up and hitched at her pants; if anyone was sober enough to notice, she wanted to give the idea she was heading for the stand of Lombardy poplar around the cabin which some of the women had been using for a latrine. Lizzie gave her a narrow look, which Chris ignored. There would be time enough for that later.

The screen door at the cabin's rear opened into a surprisingly neat kitchen. Chris eased across the room, careful not to kick anything in the dimness. She went past a cast-iron woodstove and edged along the dividing wall. At the far side a pencil line of light spilled through a chink where two logs did not quite come together, a slit about six inches long that afforded a view of most of the front sitting room.

Rock was straddling his chair in the corner, coffee cup close at hand, ebony shades reflecting the darting light of the two kerosene lamps illuminating the meeting. His cutoff was pushed back so the big Colt Peacemaker was a looming presence in its tie-down holster. Bear, in his ratty fur coat, stood behind him, sergeant-at-arms, the perfectly dull-witted bodyguard; Snake lounged on an old-fashioned overstuffed velveteen-upholstered sofa which was swaybacked from years of supporting Gigantic Gene's bulk. Rodger the Dodger of the Satan's Sons, a dark-haired Manic Mama with a badly pocked face, and three other club presidents rounded out the crew.

"The last news we heard was not cool," Rock was saying. Only his mouth moved; the rest of his face seemed never to change expression, and the rest was oddly fascinating, like watching a cleverly made robot. "Couple of months ago we got a dude called Stray Ray into the Ghetto Busters, out of Trenton—the Busters are a Mad Dog satellite club, but they handle a lot of New York City work for the Dogs, so they keep pretty close to what's happening. Anyway, Stray Ray's really a Thrillkiller, and he was getting word back to us."

"What do you mean, was?" the Mama asked.

"Couple weeks ago he walked into a bullet, face-first."

"They fingered him?"

Rock shrugged. "It doesn't much matter now—we found out what we wanted to know."

"Which is."

"We're looking at real trouble."

"Shit," Rodger the Dodger put in. "Them scumsuckers are dead meat."

Rock shook his head. "They want to kick our asses. They're figuring to take over the whole shooting match."

"Stomp the fuckers." In the kitchen, Chris shifted her position so she could see the speaker, a black guy with a Mohawk haircut.

"Why not off Apeman?" Snake drawled. "A sighted-in Winchester, a good scope, and the asshole is history."

"It's a possibility," Rock said. "But we'd be taking a chance. At best, some other dude will take over like Apeman did, and be after our asses sooner or later too. At worst, the Dogs will go batshit and start a full-on war."

"That's cool," Rodger the Dodger said complacently, as if Rock had suggested they go out and pick up some stray chicks.

"Rodger," Rock said patiently, "what are the Sons pulling in on the coyote operation?"

Rodger shrugged. "Ten, maybe twelve grand a month."

Rock looked across the room, directly at the chink through which Chris was staring. She felt her heart thump. But then Blinker appeared from the blind corner, his eyes wide behind his thick glasses. He opened a leather binder and flipped through the legal-sized pages.

"As of the last audit, our assets stood at the highest level in club history." Blinker had a precise clipped tone. "The crystal-meth operation out of Oakland netted over two hundred thousand dollars monthly over the last fiscal year, with wholesale sales to other outlets providing an additional forty-seven thousand. Regular contracted protection work for the Mafia runs around one-eighty-seven thousand a month among all clubs, and Rock recently renegotiated our per-job one-time fee for special work, raising it to a hundred and twenty thousand dollars for hits, ninety-five thousand for insurance thefts and arson, and comparable amounts for other work."

He turned a page. "At last count, satellite clubs owned through their agents and attorneys thirty-seven legitimate businesses, primarily bars but also including four pawnshops, three motorcycle dealerships, a coin-operated laundry, and a video arcade. Club personal-property assets include fourteen support vans, and last month we added another Gates Lear jet on the Colombia run. Our foreign bank accounts total just under two million, and our investment portfolio has increased in net value twenty percent in the first six months of this year to one-point-seven million, under my direction," he added with pride.

"Thanks bro," Rock cut in. "Now you got a better idea of what we stand to lose. Sure, we all love the biker life-style—but we also like good dope, and righteous living, and not having to work for the goddamned Man. We can go to war with the Mad Dogs, and maybe we can cut their nuts off. But war will be a full-time job, which means we'll have to suspend operations—and once we do that, you can bet your ass plenty of others will step in to take over. Probably we can rebuild, but that'll cost us too. So even after we fight the Mad Dogs and win, we still come up the big losers."

"And that's *if* we win," Blinker added.

Rodger stood up and began to pace angrily. "I can't believe I'm hearing this shit. In the old days we'd get a couple hundred bros, ride into the Mad Dog clubhouse, and tear their fucking arms and legs off."

"This isn't the old days." Rock's voice went cold, and

Rodger stopped abruptly. "We got three thousand bros out there right now, pulling in a couple million a month, because we spent fifteen years getting our shit together. We're not going to piss that away now because you want to kick some ass. You need trouble, Rodger, you ride into town and tear up a bar. You got me?"

For a long moment Rodger the Dodger did not move, and Chris could feel the tension vibrate in the other room. Then Rodger's shoulders slumped a little. "Aw right," he said. "So what do we do?"

"We take it easy." But Rock seemed to relax a little too. "We haven't just been sitting on our asses on this. I've been checking Apeman out. For one thing, we got the word from our wop friends that he's been stocking up on firepower—and I'm talking M16's and Ingrams, in case lots. For another, this Apeman is one insane power-hungry son of a bitch—so we got to feed him without letting him take the food off our plates.

"First thing," Rock went on, "we set up a meet. Outsiders and Mad Dogs only, enough bros to make everyone feel safe, but not so many that things are likely to blow up."

"Then we get 'em shit-faced and stomp hell out of 'em," Rodger suggested.

"Then," Rock said, "we talk alliance."

Rodger's three-hundred-pound bulk quivered as if he were making an effort to control himself. "Apeman will pull a double cross," he said, his voice tight. "You know he will."

"Sure," Rock said. "But an alliance opens up possibilities. Maybe we pull our own double cross before he has time. Maybe we can get an observer in with him, figure out more about his operation. At worst it buys us time."

That was when Chris Amado's time ran out.

A huge slab of meat clamped over her face and Gigantic Gene's fat leering face flashed in front of her eyes before he dragged her back through the kitchen and out the door. She did not try to struggle; the massive ex-biker was incredibly

90

strong, and she had no doubt he could break her spine with his bare hands. She wondered how he was able to move his bulk so silently.

By now it was full dark. Gene pulled her around, pinning her arms to her side. "Traitor bitch," he wheezed into her face. His breath stank of beer. "Ought to kill you." Light came into his deep-sunk eyes. "But first I'm gonna turn you out to the dudes."

While he was enjoying the idea, Chris brought her knee up between his legs.

But his huge stomach protected his crotch, and all she got was another wheeze of breath in the face. She tried again, and this time Gene grunted and winced slightly. Chris kicked out a third time, and twisted hard enough to get an arm free. She planted her fist in the middle of his fat face. It didn't do any visible damage, but Gene was surprised enough to loosen his grip. Chris yanked hard and got free, going down on one knee.

"You're dead meat, cunt." Gigantic Gene loomed over her, big as a mountain.

Chris pulled her Buck knife, unfolded the blade. Gigantic Gene stared at it for a moment and licked his lips as if he were about to sit down to Thanksgiving dinner. His hand disappeared into the folds of his coveralls and emerged holding his own blade. He grinned at her and closed.

The ex-biker moved with surprising grace, but Chris had speed on her side. She feinted, then stepped back and kicked up hard and high. The knife flipped out of Gigantic Gene's ham-sized mitt and stabbed into the ground a couple of feet away.

His eyes darted from her to the knife and back to her. He started to bend to pick it up.

But bending was not Gigantic Gene's strong suit. Chris foot-faked right and came in left, burying the blade in his immense gut.

His mitts came up and locked around Chris's throat.

She yanked the blade and stabbed again, and realized with a flash of despair that the guy's thick fat layer was protecting his vital organs. She went for the chest the third time, tried to get the blade between rib and muscle the fourth. His grip weakened a little—but Chris knew she was seconds from blacking out.

She got the knife up and slashed at his fat face. Flecks of blood sprinkled over her in a fine mist.

Gigantic Gene wheezed and let her go.

Chris planted the knife hilt-deep in the side of his fat neck. Blood pulsed from his severed jugular. His pig eyes widened, and then he sat down. The earth seemed to move.

Chris pulled her blade, wiped it on the dead man's overalls. She found his knife under him and planted it in the wound, then got the hell away from there.

Chapter Nine

Lizzie made a sound like a kitten drowning. She took a step back, tried to turn and got her feet tangled, and fell to all fours. Stale beer and bile spewed from her mouth and nose and splattered on the hard-packed ground of the yard behind the ranch house. Blinker couldn't hold it that long; his vomit erupted spontaneously, dribbling down the front of his T-shirt and cutoff.

"He was done with his own knife." Rock stared through his dark glasses at the mountainous mutilated body of Gigantic Gene. The corpse lay on its back like a flipped turtle, splayed legs big as tree trunks, arms like chuck roasts, all this great mound of flesh in symmetrical repose, like the object of worship at a Black Mass. Great volumes of blood, more than it seemed one body could contain, gleamed wetly in the starlight. The body looked solid and massive; it would take a D-6 Cat to move the poor dead slob.

Wee Winnie was weeping quietly. She swallowed air. "That's his knife," she confirmed, and shuddered, then began crying again, more loudly.

"Lizzie!" Rock said sharply.

The hard-faced blond woman dragged herself to her feet, wiping her mouth with the back of her hand. Her eyes were red and hollow and carefully directed away from the cadaver; the ends of her hair and the front of her shirt were damp.

Rock jutted his chin in Wee Winnie's direction. "Take care of her."

"What do you—?"

"Just get her the hell away from here."

Chris Amado, standing at the edge of the small circle of Outsiders, felt grim satisfaction. For the first time, Rock was rattled.

The Outsider president waited until Wee Winnie was out of earshot, then scanned the assembled club members. The word had gotten out, discreetly but quickly; Gene had been dead no more than twenty minutes. Chris had been tipped by Snake, who found her apparently shooting the breeze at the Jive Devils' camp.

"Zippo, Crazy George, Rat." Rock pointed out the three in turn. "Gigantic Gene's pickup truck is in the shed back there. Hoist him into the back somehow and cover him, then get him the hell out of here. I don't want him found—and if he is, I don't want him identifiable. You know what I mean. Pretty Boy, you get the support van and bring it around back here. Move it."

The four disappeared into the darkness. "A couple of you clean this blood up somehow, kick the dirt around so it doesn't show come morning. The rest of you get back out there and party like nothing happened, and keep your god-damned mouths shut about this. You dig?"

The rest of the Outsiders nodded. Someone found a garden rake and began scraping at the dark-stained ground.

"Snake, Blinker, Bear, you come with me." Rock looked around until his eyes lit on Chris. "You too, Princess."

"Sure," Chris said, trying to sound offhand.

Rock led them back to the front room of Gigantic Gene's cabin. For several minutes he scanned them from his chair in the corner without saying a word. No one else spoke either; all of them knew how serious this was. Rock's gaze ended on Chris, and he left it there for a while before finally saying, "What do you know about this, Princess?"

The disconcerting premonition chewed into her guts: somehow, he knew. Again she had that disquieting notion that he was prescient, that somehow he had peeled off her cover and recognized what was underneath.

She forced herself to shake the creepy feeling off. "Nothing you don't know." She shrugged, too elaborately. " 'Course we can all make a guess."

Rock would not rise to that bait. "Where have you been for the last hour?"

"Partying with some Jive Devil bros, down the river."

"These Devils got names?"

"Not that they mentioned," Chris drawled.

"What'd they look like?"

"Like every other scooter tramp," Chris snapped impatiently. "What are you getting at, Rock?"

He stared back at her. Bear stood impassively behind his leader, and from the corner of her eye Chris noticed Blinker's gaze flicking back and forth between them, like a spectator at a tennis match.

But then it was Rock's turn to shrug. "Forget it." He looked speculatively at Snake, who had dug up a can of beer somewhere. "Anyway, Princess is right. We've all got an idea about what happened to Gigantic Gene."

"Mad Dogs," Blinker said quietly.

"Could be someone in this camp—one of the bros—had a grudge against Gene." Snake spoke slowly, thinking out loud. "It's not impossible. But they'd have to be stone crazy to kill him now, in the middle of a run surrounded by a shitload of bros. If you wanted to off Gene, you'd show up with a squirt gun some morning when only him and Winnie were around, and pump a clip into them."

"Which means," Chris cut in, "this didn't have anything to do with Gene. He was handy, and he was an Outsider—one time, anyway. They wanted to show they could pull it off. They wanted to prove they could get to us, that they could shit on us in the middle of our own run."

Rock gave her a thoughtful look, but nodded his agreement. "They wanted to show us up, and they wanted to start trouble."

"They'll get it," Bear growled.

"Goddamned right," Snake said.

"No," Rock said quietly.

"They killed a bro," Bear said savagely. "Someone kills a bro, you stomp the fucking bastard until he's a greasy puddle."

"Listen," Rock said reasonably. "Trouble is what they want; we give it to them, and we play into their hands. If the satellite clubs find out the Dogs got into camp—and they will if we don't put a lid on this double-quick—they're gonna start worrying, maybe figure we can't protect them anymore."

"Fuck 'em." Snake stood up and pointed a finger down at Rock. "The Dogs killed Gene. We get the Dogs."

"You're jumping the gun, bro." Rock's voice was steel-hard. "You're not running this club yet." He rose fluidly and faced Snake, within the bigger man's reach. "I say no open war, at least not yet. You got me, bro?"

Snake's fists were balled at his side, and a vein was throbbing in his temple.

"You got me, bro?" Rock repeated.

Snake lowered his eyes from Rock's hidden gaze. "I got you," he mumbled. He turned away.

"Glad that's settled," Rock said levelly. "Here's the rest of the play: we step up security, but no strong-arm stuff—the party goes on. Meanwhile, I'll start setting something up with Apeman; after this we got to parley with the Dogs soon as we can."

"Parley?" Snake echoed.

"Snake, you're in charge here until the end of the run."

Snake opened his mouth and shut it again. Chris was impressed. Rock knew what he was doing: he'd let Snake know who was running the Outsiders—and then handed over the temporary reins. Snake was boxed.

"Me and Blinker and Crazy George take off tonight," Rock said, "soon as we can slip out of camp. Princess comes along."

"Okay by me," Chris said.

"What about Lizzie?" Snake asked. There was a little sneer in his voice, as if the question regained him a point or two.

"She stays with you."

"She ain't gonna like that."

Rock didn't bother to reply.

"Well, like you say," Snake went on, "you're the boss."

"Right," Rock said mildly. "Keep that in mind. You'd better see to the security detail. While you're out there, round up Crazy George. Tell him to round up our bikes and bring 'em around back—quietly."

Rock said nothing after Snake went out. Blinker shifted from one foot to the other; when Chris glanced in his direction, he stared at the floor. In five minutes, Crazy George came in, looking nervous, even more wide-eyed than usual. "I got the bikes. Pretty Boy is out back too, with the van."

It was the black panel truck that Chris had seen in the

parking lot of the Hellhole. Rock swung open the rear double doors. The dome light of the cargo area came on. Rock worked a key in the lock of a stand-up metal cabinet bolted to one wall.

Inside, a small arsenal was carefully racked, an assortment of half a dozen rifles, handguns, and one sawed off shotgun. Rock selected an Ingram M-11, jammed a thirty-two-round magazine home, and stuck the machine pistol, no bigger than a .45 automatic, into his gunbelt.

Pretty Boy stood holding open the door, leering at Chris. She turned away to check out her bike. When she glanced back, she saw Pretty Boy speaking in a low voice to Rock. Pretty Boy pointed his chin in her direction. "Not now, goddammit," Rock snapped.

He pushed past Pretty Boy and came up to her. "Saddle up, Princess," Rock said. "Time to ride."

BOOK TWO

The Iron Fist

Chapter Ten

No traffic had passed along this block of Nineteenth Street since a police car cruised by seven minutes earlier. The cop glanced incuriously at Chris Amado and drove on, as if a beautiful woman in leathers idling a stripped Harley hog was a fairly unremarkable sight in lower Manhattan.

The street was a narrow dark canyon of warehouses and loft buildings. The one across from Chris was typical: six stories high, unmarked, fronted by a loading entrance wide and high enough to admit a semi-rig.

She was wearing a watch now, a stainless-steel digital chronometer with LED readout; this part of the mission called for on-the-money timing. It was four minutes before midnight.

She had come close to eighteen hundred miles in twenty-four hours, with barely a dozen minutes to spare. It was Interstate all the way, and she'd kept the bike up against the top end, never dropping below 100 mph, more typically cruising at 120, hot prairie wind tearing at her skin and whipping back her close-cropped dark hair, the big 74-cubic-inch engine red-lined at 9500 rpm and whining like the souls of the damned. At night, truck drivers blinked as she flashed through their headlights. They reached for their CB's, then thought better of it: *Gotta stop popping them whites, Bubba, starting to see crazed women on screaming Milwaukee iron.* In the daytime, decent citizens in madras shirts and boxy Winnebagos jerked in their big captain's seats like they'd been goosed. Their eyes turned stony with righteous outrage as the chippy on the chopped motorcycle tore past and instantly out of sight, and they turned to their paint-faced wives and swore at such an affront to all that was holy. Wives murmured, "Ssssh—not in front of the children," and pretended not to recognize the sullen resentment and goatish lust which the flare of indignation failed to hide.

Somewhere in the middle of Kansas, an hour before the end of the first night, she picked up her first cop. His black-and-white was a new Chevy with a custom cop package that included a healthy herd of extra horses, and he hung on her tail for ten miles. Chris shook him when she caught up with a convoy of semis, goosing her scoot and cutting down the divider line between the row of trucks and a couple of passing cagers. There were other cops after she made the Mississippi, maybe a half-dozen in all, but there was also more traffic, so they were easier to lose. One Smokey snuck up to within a few yards of her sissy bar before hitting the siren. She cut hard left, shot across the median strip, dodged a surplus UPS van with "Jesus Died for Your Sins" written in cursive script on its side, and came back up on the right side of the Interstate with a dozen cars blocking out the cruiser.

She had nothing against the cops. They were doing their job.

But right now, her job was a hell of a lot more important.

Twenty-four hours before: from the late Gigantic Gene's ranch, Rock had led them down through Wyoming, to Denver and a topless joint on East Colfax that fronted a whorehouse run by the Manic Mamas. Chris caught two hours of sleep in one of the upstairs rooms, interrupted briefly by a fat citizen in a polyester suit who thought she was one of the girls, then interrupted permanently when Rock shook her roughly by the shoulder. He'd made contact with Apeman, he told her. Apeman had agreed to a meet with a representative of the Outsiders.

She was the representative. "Chicks up front," Rock said sardonically.

It was another test: a single day to cross two-thirds of the country, so she could walk into what was almost surely a deadly trap. Apeman would try to squeeze her until she spilled everything she knew about Rock and the Outsiders, then turn her out to the Mad Dogs—and Rock knew it. But he had little to lose. There was always the thin chance that she could actually pull it off and set up the summit between the two clubs. If not, Rock would try something else. She was dispensable.

So she was back out in the middle of the tightrope—with a pack of animals snarling and clawing for her from either end.

Chris Amado wheeled her bike around to face the warehouse across the darkened Manhattan street. She flicked on her headlight, waited two beats, turned it off-on-off-on at half-second intervals. For a minute nothing happened.

Then the garage door rolled slowly up on its tracks. Inside was dense blackness.

Chris goosed the accelerator and eased forward in low gear, bucking smoothly up over the curb and into the dark maw of the warehouse. The door clattered shut behind her, and the blackness became absolute, thick as pitch, suffocating as an asbestos curtain. She flicked off the Harley's mill and silence filled up the void like flowing wet cement. Time passed. Her eyes dilated and still she could see nothing.

She anticipated the blinding spotlights but was still disconcerted by their brilliant, painful intensity. For fifteen or twenty seconds she could not open her eyes wider than slits through which she saw nothing but harsh glary whiteness, and it was a full minute before she could make out the object in front of her face.

It was the muzzle of a suppressor, threaded over the business end of an Ingram M-10 machine pistol.

Above the Ingram's folding stock was the bearded face

of a biker. There was a razor scar under his right eye and he was grinning along the gun barrel like a schoolboy at a peephole drilled in the wall of the girls' shower room.

Chris was parked near the middle of what could have been the shipping-and-receiving department of some business engaged in light manufacturing. It was cavernous, two stories and perhaps seventy-five feet to a side; the blinding light came from banks of halide spots hung from an ironwork catwalk that ran around three sides of the room along the perimeter of the high ceiling. A half-dozen other bikers looked down from it, each of them armed with an autorifle. It was a hell of a defensive setup; Chris could have charged in backed by every Outsider in the club, and in maybe six seconds they'd be sprayed with enough lead to mold a sash weight.

Half of the room was filled with crates, stacked neatly with aisles wide enough to admit the forklift parked nearby. Several piles were of wooden boxes the size and shape of children's coffins, and were stamped "U.S. Govt. Issue." Cardboard cartons were stenciled with familiar brand names of stereos, televisions, and other electronic goods.

Across the room a dozen bikes were parked. Some were entire and looked new, others were missing seats or fenders or gas tanks. Parts, from oil pumps to entire rebuilt engines, littered the four repair bays; to one side there was a clean-room with an overhead-track compressor-fed spray gun. This was a chop-shop, where serial numbers could be filed from stolen bikes before they were refitted for resale at fifty percent of the market price.

They wanted her to see this, Chris figured. They wanted her to know how much pull they had, here in the center of the East Coast action.

The biker waggled the Ingram, as if unsure he had her complete attention. "Are you Princess?"

"No," Chris said. "I'm Jane Fucking Pauley."

Up on the catwalk someone snickered. Chris popped

down the kick stand, then threw a leg over her bike and stood facing the gunman. He blinked and took a step toward her.

Chris's hand came up from the back of her belt, holding the little four-barrel COP .357 Magnum derringer.

For a beat no one moved—and then Chris flipped the gun in her hand and held it out to the guy, flat on her palm and butt forward. "Hold this for me, would you, bro?"

The Mad Dog transferred the Ingram to his left hand, snatched up the little gun, and stashed it in a back pocket. "Now the knife," he said.

It was a deliberate insult. She had given up the pistol willingly, and the knife was no threat. She was surrounded by heavy hardware, and no doubt would be until she left this place—or died.

"Go fuck yourself."

"The knife, mama." He held out his right hand.

Chris's heavy biker boot shot up in a dancer's kick, and the heel caught him at the point of his nose. He went down as if he'd been shot, the Ingram tumbling from nerveless fingers. Blood bubbled from the middle of his face but he did not move, and Chris wondered if she'd killed him. A blow like that, to the weakest part of the skull, could drive shards of bone into the frontal lobes.

Chris stepped over him and looked up at the bikers on the catwalk. Every weapon was trained on her, every eye watching, every mouth open. "What's the goddamned story?" Chris hollered. "Are we doing business?"

"That's right, Princess."

The man standing behind her was well built and might have been darkly handsome, except for the grotesque blue tattoo in the shape of a mask that covered his face from forehead to cheekbone. "Like it, Princess?" he asked. "I got to smoking some righteous KW one night, and you know how it is. You smoke that angel dust, you get ideas. I thought this was a good one. Hope you do like it, 'cause I go about halfway crazy when chicks mouth off about it."

"Halfway is about as far as you've got to go."

He surprised her by laughing. "Come on, Princess. Places want us to go to them." She got a look at the Mad Dogs' colors when he turned: a vicious rabid snarling canine, more wolf than dog, with "Mad Dogs MC" stitched above it.

The biker pulled back a metal accordion gate in the back wall and gestured her into the freight elevator. He watched her as the cage rose, picking at his teeth with a dirty thumbnail. Chris ignored him and stared through the gate. They passed three floors. She glimpsed other warehouse spaces, a hallway off which doors opened on either side.

The tattooed guy cranked the lever and the elevator creaked to a stop. Two armed bikers flanked a door. They stepped aside to let Chris push through. The tattooed guy followed her into the double-interlock chamber; it was the size of a large closet; the TV camera mounted on a gimbal in one corner of the ceiling scanned them. A relay clicked, and the lock of the inner door snicked open.

The room on the other side was as out of place in this building as a stripper at a Holy Communion. It could have been the office of a corporation executive. A window draped with heavy velour, parted enough to show a panoramic view of lower Manhattan, dominated one wall. The others were covered by high bookshelves and fine art. There was a thick soft leather-upholstered sofa and two matching chairs, a hardwood coffee table, a few plants, a couple of floor lamps with curled toes on their brass bases, a thick earth-colored rug.

The desk facing Chris across the room was hand-crafted out of hardwood polished to a perfect shine. Its high-backed chair faced away from them.

"Here's the Outsider mama, bro," the tattooed biker announced.

The chair swiveled slowly around. Chris started to say something—and then just stood there, her mouth half-open.

The man who rose from the chair was the most grotesque human being she had ever seen.

His head was huge and simian, with a high sloping forehead that ended in a scarified ridge covered with eyebrows that formed a single unseparated line of black fur. His hair was long, black, and thickly matted, and his beard matched, framing thick lips that were an odd shade of bright red. His eyes were black as well, as small and unblinking as .22-caliber slugs, devoid of human reason or emotions beyond the most elemental, like pain and lust; they were the eyes of a lower order of beast, where animal cunning and brute strength prevailed over rationality. He was as wide as a door, with sloping shoulders ropy with muscle, thick arms that seemed to hang nearly to his knees, a trunk like a fifty-five-gallon drum, and a bulging hard stomach. He stank. An odor of dirt and decay rose from him in waves and drifted to the corners of the room.

He wore an immaculate gray suit with matching vest, a conservative rep tie, and a hog-leg .45 in a holster on his hip.

"Meet Apeman, bitch," the tattooed biker said. It sounded like an order.

Apeman stared at her, and Chris watched a gross goatish smile part his gargoyle features. His mouth opened, and Chris gasped.

His teeth were filed to sharp points.

Apeman wiped his mouth with the sleeve of his suit coat. His red lips glistened. "New meat," he growled hungrily.

Chapter Eleven

"Crenshaw," Charley Benjamin said thoughtfully. He snapped his fingers. "Sure, I remember the bastard. They called him Creepshow back then."

"Here's the printout on him." Miss Paradise handed over a sheaf of fan-fold computer paper. "We got it from a contact we have in the Organized Crime Unit of the New York State attorney general's office."

"What about Apeman?" Dennison asked.

"There's not much on him. It's appended at the end."

Charley Benjamin scanned the data sheets. Miss Paradise stood at the railing of the porch that fronted Dennison's headquarters. She wore a white T-shirt, yellow satin jogging shorts, and sandals; her impossibly long legs were bronzed, the calf and thigh muscles cleanly defined. A half-empty pack of Marlboros and a disposable Bic lighter were rolled up in the T-shirt's sleeve.

The midsummer day was unusually warm, even at the mile-plus altitude of Dennison's compound. The porch looked out over an expanse of green lawn, about fifty yards on a side, brilliantly green and freshly mowed by Dennison the day before; each year he insisted on taking charge of the gardening chores at the compound. Miss Paradise called it his therapy.

At the far edge of the clearing a ten-foot pole supported a bright orange windsock, which stirred lazily in the gentle summer breeze. A Bell Model 222 Executive helicopter was parked beside it. Aside from a four-day hike that was close to a technical rock-climb in places, the chopper was the only way into the compound. Heavy evergreen forest surrounded the clearing, dense with lodgepole pine, blue spruce, and quaking aspen, thick virgin growth that had never been logged or even thinned. It sloped away in front of the building, gently for a few hundred yards, then much more steeply, dropping two thousand feet to the creek cascading between steep rock walls in the valley below.

Behind Dennison's headquarters the mountain slope became cliff. The tree line was five hundred feet above, and the last one thousand feet to the summit was a vertical face of crumbling granite narrowing to a sharp pinnacle. It was occupied by a twenty-foot steelwork tower anchored by guy wires strung to eyebolts drilled into solid rock; on the tower were two antennae and a microwave dish mounted on a remote-controlled directional rotor. Beside the tower, aimed at the southern sky, was a satellite receiver. It had nothing to do with the compound's communications network, but Miss Paradise enjoyed television, and Dennison enjoyed pleasing her.

An old logging road was visible on the far ridge, but it hadn't been used for a decade. Its access was on the other side, nearly forty land miles from the compound, where it was blocked by a six-foot ditch, according to the terms of an easement Dennison held under the name of a cousin who had been dead for seventeen years. In the one thousand square miles of territory visible from Dennison's vantage point, there were no other signs of civilization or human encroachment.

The building housed offices for Dennison and Miss Paradise, the communications/computer center they called the Back Room, and accommodations for the operatives and clients whom Dennison coptered in when necessary. It was angular and multifaceted, all redwood shakes, stained pine trim, and tinted glass shaped into something a child might have built by randomly gluing together a dozen prismatic boxes. The design was deliberate: for one thing, it concealed the interior layout like a magician's fast-handed misdirection; for another, if someone stumbled into the compound or happened to overfly it, it would look like nothing more than a lodge or cabin put up by someone with more money than taste.

The compound had cost a great deal to build, and continued to cost a great deal to run. Dennison was not a rich man, although he could have been several times over. He enjoyed certain comforts, but wealth did not interest him. Money was a necessity, and always easily available. There were more than enough rich men in the world willing to support Dennison's operation by paying for his services.

Dennison was a mercenary. When the job was dangerous or difficult, when the authorities were handcuffed by rules and regulations and red tape, Dennison got it done. Dennison's fee was from one-quarter of a million dollars up, depending on the job and the client, payable in advance.

Most clients were wealthy; that simplified Dennison's business. Rich people expected to pay dearly for special service, and Dennison always gave them their money's worth. Once a mission began, Dennison had carte blanche, including sole authority to decide when the mission was successfully complete. He did not give refunds—but then, he had never been asked for one.

Dennison fought a war of containment. He had no illusions about curing the world; he was satisfied if he could occasionally disinfect some small part of it.

Right now, two bands of soulless animals were about to sit down at a table to try to carve up the country like a Christmas ham.

Dennison planned to stop them.

It was no more complex or mystic than that. There had been a time when Dennison was associated with certain sanctioned agencies, when he had played by the intricate rules of law and procedure and due process. As near as he could tell, those rules were designed according to the same logic by which weights were assigned in a handicapped thoroughbred stakes race.

The only problem was that as soon as they got in the starting gate, the bad guys slipped their weights. The cops knew it—and there wasn't a damned thing they could do.

Dennison didn't have that problem. He played by the same rules as the savages, which were no rules at all. The Mad Dogs and the Outsiders and all the other hoodlums in the biker nation were killers; for two decades they had been stomping anyone who got in their way. Once their nationwide alliance was in place, they'd be the most powerful criminal organization in the world.

Dennison knew you did not fight scum like the bikers with law. You did not arrest them and arraign them and try them before a jury of their so-called peers, so some lawyer with the moral conviction of a turkey buzzard could get them off with probation or a fine. You fought them with fists and knives and guns, the same weapons they used.

You stomped the bastards into bloody meat.

Dennison could not do it alone; the enemy were too strong, and there was too much at stake. Over the years he had developed a network of free-lance operatives, an elite corps of professional warriors with unique skills, on call at all times, ready to take on whatever work Dennison provided. Dennison paid them one hundred thousand dollars per assignment, plus expenses. They were worth every penny.

Dennison's People were the ones who entered the den of the beast and faced the monster head to head, and Dennison never lost sight of the fact. Now, sitting on the shaded porch in a well-used cane-and-canvas lounger, sipping from a tall glass filled with a shot of Martell five-star brandy and soda over crushed ice, Dennison was thinking of Chris Amado. He did not waste worry on her; she was a warrior, and in any case worry only warped judgment. But he felt the constant vague knot in the pit of his gut, and knew it would not unclench until the mission was complete and she returned from the belly of the brute, entire and unscarred.

At the railing, Miss Paradise unrolled the Marlboros and lifted a cigarette between long fingernails. Dennison watched her smoke: she took short impatient puffs, as if she did not really enjoy it. Her translucently pale blond hair glistened in the sunlight with impossible radiance; the thin material of the T-shirt outlined the nipples of her small high breasts. He had lived a lifetime—one of his lifetimes, at least—with this extraordinary woman, and yet he never looked at her without being struck again by her breathtaking beauty. He could not contemplate life without her, or anyway did not wish to.

Charley Benjamin finished scanning the printout. "You figure Creepshow Crenshaw is Apeman now?"

Dennison pointed his chin at Miss Paradise. From his earlier days in the spook world of sanctioned agencies, Dennison had contacts across the country and around the world. He knew when to do a favor and when to call in a debt. So he made the calls and asked the questions—but Miss Paradise was in charge of the computerized intelligence analysis that was the necessary follow-up.

"There's a ninety-five-percent probability," Miss Paradise said. "The problem is that all the correlations are objective—age, height, weight, known association with mobsters, the usual. None of the intel on Crenshaw is more recent than three years back, and none of the dope on Apeman in older than two. So there's a degree of potential of error on this one, boss."

Benjamin shook his head. "It's the same guy."

"You know that?" Dennison asked.

"In my gut." Benjamin pinched at the bridge of his nose. "I ran into this Creepshow four years back, at a Fourth of July run to Weirs Beach, on Lake Winnepesaukee in New Hampshire. He was president of the Breeds, a club out of Revere Beach, north of Boston. Everyone was afraid of him, even the other bikers—hell, even the other Breeds. Most presidents are at least halfway shrewd; they've got to be to deal with business while keeping their members in line. But Creepshow dealt with everyone the same way: pure brute force."

"The way I hear it," Miss Paradise said, "none of those bastards are into tender loving care."

"Creepshow was different," Charley Benjamin said. "No biker needs much excuse to fight, but most won't start one for no reason at all. There's no percentage in picking mindless punchouts, because sooner or later you're the one who gets punched out.

"Creepshow was operating on a different wavelength. For one thing, he was a genuine bully—he got a kick out of other people's pain, especially if he could get them in the back. For another, he could get away with it. He was big and mean enough to take on anyone. He wasn't afraid because he forgot to think about fear. He was too busy trying to kill the other guy with his hands."

"Okay," Dennison said. "But what makes you so sure Creepshow is now operating as Apeman?"

"I heard the stories and the rumors before I split from the Satan's Sons. It was the same thing all over again: this Apeman dude was the meanest son of a bitch in biker history; he'd fight or fuck anything that moved." Benjamin colored slightly. "Pardon the language," he said to Miss Paradise.

She knew he was still trying to come out of the other life he had lived for too long. She smiled. "Forget it—and welcome back to the real world."

"Thanks. In any case," he went on, "Apeman is Creepshow, or his clone. It doesn't matter—except that if Chris gets too close to the bastard, it's about a sure thing she'll get burned."

Dennison had already figured that part out, and it didn't make him feel easier about this mission to hear it said out loud.

"On that Weirs Beach run . . ." Charley Benjamin cut himself off abruptly. He looked from Dennison to Miss Paradise and shook his head. "I told them at Justice, and they didn't believe me. It hadn't been reported to the police, so it hadn't happened. My God," he spat.

"Tell it, Charley," Miss Paradise said gently.

"We've got to have it all," Dennison said.

Benjamin drew a long shuddering breath. "In the old days there was a biker catch phrase: 'Let's go make someone

113

a mama.' That's where the term 'mama' comes from, for a woman who . . .'' He looked at Miss Paradise again.

"Who hangs out with the club and makes it anytime with anyone who wants her."

"That's right. They're pretty sad women, most of them, the kind who've been kicked around so long they don't know any other life. Some seem to thrive on abuse; it's a way of setting up a defense. One time I saw two clubs each put up one of their mamas as the stake in a bike race. The winner club rode off with the loser's mama, and she was laughing as hard as any of them."

"Weirs Beach," Dennison reminded.

"Yeah," Charley Benjamin said bleakly. "I remember Weirs Beach."

Originally the girl had come on to the Hammerheads. She called herself Mae—Benjamin remembered that for some reason—and although she could not have been much older than twenty, she looked like she'd been around and knew what she was getting into. She had the tiny breasts and the hips of a boy, and limp brown hair; needle tracks decorated the inside of both arms and in defiance of the summer sun she had the ashen skin of the longtime junkie. She was looking for real men, she said.

Before anything could get going, Creepshow muscled into the scene. If she wanted men, she wanted the Breeds. He yanked her off down the street before she thought about arguing.

You did not walk off with another club's mama—but none of the Hammerheads were going to make an issue of it. They all knew about Creepshow—and no mama was worth getting your head busted. The junkie girl didn't seem worried; hell, she was there to make it with bikers, and one was as good—or bad—as the next.

But Creepshow had something to prove; he always had something to prove. He turned her out to the rest of the

Breeds, and he made a carnival out of it. They staked her out in the middle of the main street, in front of the hot-dog stands and the arcades and the popcorn wagon, and they did her one by one, or in pairs or threesomes or quartets. The local cops had surrendered the town as soon as the bikers roared in; anyone stupid enough to mess with the bastards could cover his own ass.

The girl began to scream by the time the third guy rammed inside her, and she went on screaming longer than most of them, even after they started beating her, first with open palms and then with fists and finally with their chain-drive belts.

They took a long time before they were finished with her, and by then she was only moaning and weeping and trying to draw herself into a protective ball. Creepshow stood over her and laughed for a while. Then he drew his Buck knife, pulled out the six-inch blade, and knelt in the street over her.

"He took his time," Charley Benjamin told Dennison and Miss Paradise, his voice tight. "He wiped away the blood after each letter to make sure he got them right. When he had carved out his name he laughed. No one else moved and the girl was passed out from the pain, so that was all you could hear, Creepshow giggling like a madman. I can hear it right now."

"All right," Dennison said evenly.

"No, Dennison. It is not all right."

"We'll take him out," Dennison said. "Count on it."

Benjamin screwed his eyes up tight, trying to shut out the vision of Creepshow and the wannabee mama lying there bleeding in the middle of the New Hampshire street.

"I almost forgot," Miss Paradise changed the subject smoothly. "Chicken Charley the Child Molester is dead."

"How did he get it?" Dennison asked.

"Ran off a one-lane dirt-road bridge and fell one hundred and twenty feet into the Rio Grande gorge south of Taos.

He was delivering a load of methamphetamine; the New Mexico state cops found a half-pound of ninety-five-percent-pure strapped to his sissy bars. From the length of the skid marks, they figure he was going about a hundred, probably cranked to the gills on the stuff himself."

"What about a body?"

"No problem. Unofficially, the cops told Bill Price they weren't spending good money to look for the corpse of a creep like that. Hell, Chicken Charley was on the surveillance list of every force in the Southwest. Good riddance to rubbish, they told Bill. They hoped he washed up somewhere so the coyotes and vultures could pick him clean before he polluted the Gulf of Mexico."

"Are we clean?"

"As an expurgated edition," Miss Paradise affirmed.

"Get in touch with Bill and Vang, would you?" Dennison said. "Tell them thanks and good work."

Miss Paradise started inside, but when Charley Benjamin stood and offered his hand to Dennison, she waited. Dennison rose and took it.

"I owe you, Dennison."

Dennison shook his head. "The way I remember, it's the other way around."

Miss Paradise frowned. "I was wondering about that." But then she caught Dennison's warning look and shut up. "Price and Vang. Right boss," she said crisply, and turned to give them one last look at her incredible legs before disappearing inside.

Chapter Twelve

Apeman's laugh was a threat of imminent violence, like the chatter of a rattlesnake's tail or the warning gnar of a big jungle cat. The laugh was a low-pitched chuffa-chuffa, punctuated when he drew breath by a basso gargling noise like a death rattle. The pupils of his tiny pig eyes contracted, and they glowed with the light of demonic possession. Spittle flew from his mouth; his pointed teeth were the color of a barroom floor.

Chris Amado stared at him and tried to ignore the fingernail of ice scraping up the ridge of her spine.

The slim biker with the mask tattooed across his face perched his butt on one corner of the desk. "Diablo," Apeman said in a soft warning voice, though his laughter went on unabated. Diablo did not respond; he was watching Chris with a faint grin, like a spectator awaiting the start of a dog fight.

Still laughing, Apeman leaned forward and grabbed Diablo under the armpit. With one hand he yanked the slim biker off his desk and threw him about four feet in Chris's direction. Chris stepped aside and he went past. Diablo, no longer grinning, picked himself up and went to a neutral corner.

The third Mad Dog in the room chuckled. He lay on the dark leather couch with his black biker boots propped up on one arm and watched Chris through soft dark sleepy eyes. He had skin the color of the upholstery, and had to be six and a half feet tall; his bare black arms were thick with the perfectly proportioned muscles of a weight lifter. He wore his hair in a huge bushy Afro.

Chris waited. As long as she was inside the lair of this crew of butchers, she was living moment to moment on wits, savvy, and a dose of luck. She was subject to Apeman's demented whimsy; she could make every right move and still die.

Apeman took a bottle of beer from a half-size refrigerator at the head end of the sofa. He yanked the cap off and guzzled down the contents in one noisy gulp, then tossed the bottle over his shoulder. It rolled across the thick carpet without breaking. Chris wondered who had the job of cleaning up after the slob; it would be like trying to keep a horse pasture free of shit. Yet the bizarrely out-of-character business suit somehow remained immaculate.

Apeman belched. "What you want, mama?"

"I want to do you a favor, bro."

"I ain't your bro."

"I'm not your mama."

The black man on the couch chuckled again. He lay there languid as a house cat, but his perfectly toned body broadcast a spring-loaded tension. It told Chris that he could be upright and on her in a fraction of a heartbeat.

Apeman's thick furry single eyebrow creased in a V. "What you doing here?"

"You talked to Rock," Chris said. She kept her voice neutral. "You know he wants to set up a meet with you. I'm here to show good faith. I'm trusting you. That means you can trust us, too." Simple declarative sentences; she hoped they got through.

"Why does Rock want a meet?"

"To talk."

"About what?"

"Peace between the clubs, the Outsiders and the Mad Dogs."

Diablo had slipped into a chair opposite the couch. "We've got peace now." Apeman shot him a look but did not contradict him.

"That's right," Chris said. "That's how everyone wants it, and that's how it should be." She took a couple of steps deeper into the room. "Look, we're all in the same business, and there's plenty of work—and plenty of money—to spread around. We got a good deal now, Outsiders and Mad Dogs both. We're bros, and Rock wants to keep it that way. If we get it together, we can make things even better. We can help each other in plenty of ways. We can cover each other's asses."

"I watch out for myself," Apeman said.

"That so?" Chris nodded at the sofa. "So what's Black Beauty doing, giving the couch a workout?"

Apeman sank back into his executive's swivel chair and scratched vigorously at his beard; Chris imagined body lice scurrying for cover. "How would it be," Apeman said gonially, "if I turn you out to the rest of the Dogs? We wouldn't kill you or nothin', just maybe fuck hell out of you and then cut you up some, before we ship you back to Rock. You think he'd figure out what our answer was?"

They could do it. They could do any damned thing they wanted to her, and fix it so no one would ever find the pieces.

"No good, Apeman," Chris said. Her voice was steady as an anvil. "All that's going to do, besides getting your rocks off, is make a lot of trouble. I'm a blooded member of the Outsiders. I'm a bro, whether you like it or not, and if you come down on me the Outsiders will have to kick back on you. That's the rules. If you want to start a war, go ahead. I guess I'll be the first one to die. But after that a lot of bros are going to follow me straight to hell."

"More for me," Apeman grunted.

"Jesus Christ," Chris snorted. "Rock doesn't have to talk to you—he's offering you a break. But you wouldn't recognize a good deal if it bit you in the dick, you stupid shit."

Apeman's button eyes turned cold and feral. The black man was standing up, arms relaxed at his side. Chris had not seen him move. He wore an expression of doggish eagerness. Off to the side, Diablo pushed his chair back out of the way.

"Big Buck," Apeman said.

"Yeah, boss." The black man spoke in a soft-edged pleasantly modulated drawl.

Sweat leaked from Chris Amado's pores and dribbled in chill streams down her sides.

"Do her," Apeman said.

Chris looked at the towering black man and knew she was going to die.

And thought: *Goddammit, no!* You did not give up—if anything, Dennison had taught her that. There was a measure of futility to every battle, but you did not recognize it, did not admit it into the arena. You kept defeat out of the realm of personal possibility.

She stepped back, pulled her blade, and dropped into the textbook knife-fighting crouch. Big Buck stood relaxed and ready. Chris feinted and lunged, coming in low and slashing at a target an inch below his bare navel.

Her right wrist exploded in a flash of fiery pain and her fingers lost sensation. She had time to notice the knife lying on the carpet before another bolt exploded in her shoulder and her entire arm went numb.

"Yeah." Somewhere off to the side, Diablo breathed the word with absorbed admiration, like a rube at a freak show.

Chris circled back, working for position to use her left arm. The bastard was damned good, but she'd had some martial-arts training too.

Big Buck came up with his right foot, but she dodged it—and realized too late that the move was a suck. Her weight was already moving the other way, directly into a chop to the back of her neck. For a moment she could not see, and then he hook-kicked her and she went down backward, her head bouncing off the rug.

She felt the nap of the thick carpet against her hands, and she could see the ceiling directly above, and out of her peripheral vision, Big Buck's legs.

She tried to move and could not.

Apeman's ghoulish laugh filled the room.

"Talk to me, boss," Big Buck drawled.

"Finish it."

Big Buck screamed a high-pitched "aiyeeeeee" that jabbed painful needles into Chris Amado's eardrums. She managed to turn her head. Big Buck crouched and launched himself five feet into the air in a high-stomp arc. Chris tried to roll, and incredibly, the guy adjusted in midair. Everything seemed slow-motion.

Big Buck's boots came down on either side of Chris Amado's head, so close that strands of her short hair pulled out and snapped. The floor shuddered under the impact. The black hiker stood there, holding her head cradled almost gently between boot leather.

His shiny dark face loomed before hers. "You lucky, mama. Boss must like you. He gimme the signal."

He offered his hand. Chris reached it with some effort and let him pull her to her feet. She had to grab his arm to steady herself, but she did not go down. Feeling was returning to her limbs. Big Buck nodded his satisfaction, like a concerned older brother.

"You aw right now, mama," he said, with genuine goodwill.

Chris smiled and nodded and drove her fist into his jaw. It was like punching a concrete wall. His head moved about a centimeter.

Big Buck rubbed at the spot, as if gauging whether he needed a shave. He shook his head with something like awe. "Mama, you are one crazy white chick."

Apeman was still laughing, and even Diablo had joined in now.

"All right," Chris Amado said. "If everyone is finished comparing cocks, maybe we can get down to business."

Chapter Thirteen

From his oversized office window Dennison watched the trailing edge of the sun dip below the far ridge, leaving horizontal swirls of orange and yellow and purple sunset in its wake. The evening before, there had been an aurora borealis, brilliant greenish curtains of light twisting and whirling in the northern sky, staging a private performance that he and Miss Paradise watched from the porch. The northern lights appeared only every couple of years at this latitude, but Dennison had a hunch they'd see them again that night.

"I talked to Vang and Price." Miss Paradise was in one of the comfortable old-fashioned chairs facing Dennison's desk, her long legs curled up under her. "Their checks are in the mail, as the saying goes."

Dennison went to the mantelpiece of the big stonework fireplace. He built two drinks, working carefully and deliberately: ice cubes tonged from an insulated covered bucket, then a precise shot of Martell five-star brandy, finally soda water from a siphon. He handed one tall glass to Miss Paradise and sat down behind the desk with his own.

"And speaking of checks . . ." Miss Paradise said.

"Ask your question."

"So okay," Miss Paradise said, and drank. "So maybe it's none of my business."

Dennison waited.

"The thing is, boss dear, Dennison's People is not a branch of the United Way." She fished out a cigarette. Dennison leaned across the cluttered desk and excavated the ashtray and the heavy green-glass table lighter. Miss Paradise tapped the unlit cigarette on a fingernail, then studied it critically.

"You owe him," she said finally, not looking up.

"Right," Dennison said. "I owe him."

The Son Tay job had been bad news from the start. For one thing, it was a hurry-up mission. For another, the Agency and MI had gotten into one of their typical squabbles over who was going to handle it. And for a third, after the Agency won the argument the Army insisted on handling logistics and support. Dennison had to pull Agency rank, and he knew that left a bad taste in I Corps's mouth. He didn't think they'd pull the rug from under him out of spite—but men had died for stupider reasons.

The Browning High-Power Auto Rifle was chambered for 7mm Remington Magnum rounds; the cartridge in its breech was a hollow-point hot load. Dennison nestled the butt against his right shoulder and sighted through the Litton 4X passive-light nightscope at the detention-camp compound. He scanned the open courtyard, four hundred meters distant. Near its center was a bare wooden platform, raised a couple of feet above the barren dirt. A soldier in an NVA uniform sat on the edge, his AK-47 on his knees, his chin drowsing on his chest. He was the only sign of life.

Dennison checked the luminous dial of his watch: 0145 hours. He swore softly in the darkness. The Agency had gotten word of the press conference from a Swedish journalist named Lind who reported for Reuters out of Hanoi and free-lanced for several Western intelligence services. Lind passed the info to a North Korean deputy consul who doubled for the U.S. on the side, and the Korean had broadcast a coded message to a USN destroyer working outside the fifteen-mile limit off Haiphong, which had passed it on to MI in Saigon. MI knew the Agency monitored all of its broadcast traffic, just as MI monitored the Agency, so they were unsurprised but no happier than usual when the Agency bulled its way in.

Three months earlier, a USAF bird colonel named Edward Randall had ejected over Hanoi. An NVA squad found him within an hour; he'd shattered a kneecap on the edge of the cockpit when the charge under his ass went off. He ended up in the hands of a Cong major named Giap, a first cousin of Vo Nguyen Giap, the North Vietnamese military commander-in-chief. The Agency knew that the lesser Giap was ambitious, and jealous of his cousin.

Giap began working on Randall as soon as he got his hands on the American pilot. Randall didn't see a doctor for three weeks, and then the gangrenous limb was amputated below the thigh. Randall was tortured, put through various sensory-deprivation routines, and fed a pharmacopoeia of mood-altering drugs, until Giap decided he was sufficiently docile to be used.

The day before, according to Lind, Giap had invited the foreign press corps to a special briefing at the Son Tay camp where Randall was being held. There the American colonel would relate the truth about the atrocities routinely committed by his imperialist invader comrades in the U.S. Armed Forces, and would deliver a personal confession, a description and condemnation of his own war crimes, and a plea for leniency.

Neither the Agency nor MI could expect to get the poor bastard out before Giap turned him into his ventriloquist's dummy. Dennison had come up with the next-best idea: assassinate Giap in front of the reporters. It was a half-assed solution, but they were fighting a half-assed war. At least it would postpone Giap's circus, and embarrass Hanoi.

If the damned thing came off.

Dennison swore again. He did not relish the possibility of having to return another night. Son Tay was less than twenty-five miles from Hanoi; the chances of living through this kind of assignment were unattractive at best, and decreased geometrically with each attempt.

It was 0150 hours now. Dennison was raising the scope again when his support man whispered, "To the left. Front gate."

Dennison swept the Litton in that direction. The gate swung open. Four 4WD rigs entered, headlights out. The drivers were NVA, but the passengers were civilian, mostly Caucasian. The rigs pulled around in front of the platform. The reporters piled out, and the broadcast technicians began to unload television and newsreel equipment from the back.

"Bingo," Dennison said softly.

"A piece of cake," the other man said. "So far."

Dennison looked over. Charley Benjamin was wearing the same blousy cammie fatigues as Dennison, with no insignia indicating his rank of Special Forces sergeant. In the dark cosmetic that covered both their faces, Benjamin looked older than his twenty years. Dennison had used him before.

Seconds ticked by like faint heartbeats and turned into minutes. There was a partial cloud cover, and Dennison wasn't sure if it was thickening or blowing past. Benjamin nudged him and pointed and said, "That's him."

Giap was a compact man. Flanked by two aides, he walked with a slight limp. The left chest of his jacket was tiled with battle ribbons. The murmur of the reporters drifted up the hillside to Dennison's position. An NVA grunt set up a microphone stand and ran a cord off toward one of the buildings. A translator in civvies waited in front of it.

Giap mounted the platform and clapped his hands, then launched into his act. It was the usual propaganda crap. Change the names and biases, and Westmoreland could have used it.

Spotlights mounted on two of the guard turrets at the corners of the razor-wire-topped compound wall came to life and picked out a knot of guards coming out of the building. Randall was in their midst, pulling himself along on a pair of homemade crutches. At the platform's edge a guard prodded him with his rifle butt, and Giap bent and dragged him roughly up. In the spotlight's unnatural glare Randall looked gray-faced. He could not have weighed over 130 pounds, and his head was shaved. The right leg of his dirty pajamas was tied off.

Giap jerked him in front of the microphone. Dennison framed Giap's face in the scope. The bastard was grinning.

Randall said, "I am Colonel Edward James Randall, United States Air Force. My serial number is 002-38-4802-FV."

Dennison stroked the trigger of the Browning and Giap's head exploded.

Dennison kept the scope on Giap for the few seconds it took to confirm the kill. The reporters were scattering for cover. A camera tripod toppled and smashed. Randall looked down at Giap's bleeding corpse but did not otherwise react. The spotlight turned in Dennison's direction, but by then he and Benjamin were up and dogtrotting over the ridge of the hill. Its mass cut off the confused sounds from the camp.

They went through dense jungle for the first mile and a half, before they made trail. From there it was another two miles to the LZ. It was 0235; they had twenty-five minutes to make it. Dennison led them under the canopy of jungle at a hard jog. He heard Benjamin's steady breathing behind him, the soft clink of his M16 joggling on the web belt slung over his shoulder.

Thirty seconds after they reached the edge of the LZ, Dennison heard the whap-whap of the Huey coming in. A few seconds after that, its spotlight came alive and raked the jungle clearing.

Another few seconds passed, and all hell broke loose.

Ground fire erupted across the clearing. Dennison could make out three separate clusters of muzzle flash. It was a set-up—the sons of bitches must have spotted them coming in, three hours earlier.

The Huey's door gunner opened up with his 7.62mm minigun—but the chopper would not be able to make the pickup without ground support.

Charley Benjamin pulled two HE grenades from belt clips and handed one to Dennison. "You go right," Dennison said.

"On three."

"Roger. Watch the minigun fire. He won't be able to tell who the good guys are until he gets us in the light."

The grenades' reports tore the night, followed by unholy yowls of pain. By then Dennison was moving. Two NVA infantrymen came into the clearing ten yards down the perimeter and Dennison put a six-shot burst across their guts without breaking his stride. He pushed into the undergrowth in time to see two others turn toward the sound of the return fire. They died trying to bring their AK's up. Twenty yards to the right Benjamin's M16 sounded and bodies thumped into foliage. The ground fire was sporadic now. The Huey started to come in again.

"Go!" Dennison hollered, and hit the clearing.

He was halfway to the chopper when the slug slammed into the back of his thigh. Dennison stumbled but managed to keep his feet. The second bullet hit low in his back. The Huey was three yards away, hovering a foot above the grass. Dennison lurched toward the runner and went down on his face. He knew he was hit badly, yet there was no pain.

The chopper started to rise again.

Dennison turned his head and an NVA swam into his vision near the tree line. He raised his AK and sighted at Dennison. Dennison smelled burnt powder and his own blood.

The NVA fell away backward into the brush. Hands grabbed Dennison under the armpits and lifted him. Charley Benjamin said something; Dennison could make out the voice but not the words. Dennison was standing up. There was no more shooting.

The pain finally came when they hoisted him into the Huey, and then it was so intense that Dennison went immediately away from there, into some frightening place that was black as eternity.

"Gee, boss," Miss Paradise said lightly, "I thought that mark below your butt was a dimple." She was standing behind his chair, stroking his temples. "I don't want you chasing around like that anymore," she went on with mock sternness. "You're too old to be dodging bullets."

"Maybe." Dennison sighed. He looked back over his shoulder at her. "But anyway, you see how it is with Charley and me."

"Yeah, boss dear," she murmured. "I see how it is."

Chapter Fourteen

A couple of entries down from the unmarked garage door on Nineteenth Street, a woman's legs stuck out of a trash dumpster. The legs depended from under a flower-print cotton dress, were encased in thick beige support hose that did not entirely hide an abstract map of varicose veins, and ended in ballet pumps with holes in the soles. It was soon after the early-summer dawn, and the first rays of the sun to reach between the buildings were climbing up the side of the dumpster toward the legs.

The legs wiggled and ascended from the trash, followed by the rest of the flower-print dress, which encased the dumpy shapeless body of a middle-aged woman with gray hair stiff as steel wool and bifocals with one cracked lens. She wrestled a plastic bag out after her. Aluminum cans clinked.

Across the street in the shelter of a recessed doorway, a young black man opened his eyes and immediately began to shiver violently, although it was already at least seventy degrees. He pulled a long-sleeved woolen peacoat around his neck and drew into it like a turtle, began rummaging around in the pockets from the inside.

The bag lady stopped to watch a sanitation-department street-sweeping truck cruise by, sluicing water along the curb. She waved at the driver listlessly. He ignored her. A bread truck passed in the other direction. The junkie came fully awake and began to moan.

The unmarked garage door clattered up on its rollers. The sound was too harsh for the early hour, and when it stopped the silence seemed deeper and more portentous. The bag lady cocked her head to one side, as if tuned to a frequency only she could hear.

From within the dimness beyond the opening came the thick throaty rumbling of a motor, and then another and another, building to a roaring, pulsing crescendo. The junkie licked his lips and stopped moaning. The bag lady dropped her sack of cans and clapped both hands over her ears.

Apeman came shooting from the door as if vomited from the gullet of some monstrous vulture. He sat astride a jet-black Harley fatbob, chopped and radically raked, twin pipes belching black exhaust. He wore his immaculate three-piece business suit with his Colt .45 strapped on over it. He stopped the bike in the middle of the deserted street and revved the motor for the pure evil joy of hearing the unholy scream of it echo up and down the canyon of buildings.

The bag lady turned and ran in the other direction, her cheap cotton dress swirling around her stocky legs. Her abandoned sack toppled over, and crushed cans dribbled into the gutter.

Side by side, Diablo and Big Buck shot out of the garage and formed up behind Apeman. Other Mad Dogs followed, stylized as a regimental parade, until fifteen pairs of eager bikers formed a precise two-column formation in the middle of the street. The junkie blinked and tried to make himself invisible in the doorway, and forgot for a moment how junk-sick he was.

Chris Amado on her silver-cloud chopper came through the door, and it clattered shut behind her.

Apeman turned in his saddle and looked over his congregation. He nodded, and then his monkey face screwed up in his version of a grin of approval. He faced front again, raised his left fist, and held for a moment, as if posing for the photographic record of a historical event.

Then he red-lined in first gear and popped the clutch. His Harley reared up on its back wheels and took off like that, the hot exhaust of his tailpipes drawing parallel lines of black on the pavement for twenty yards. The others followed, always in pairs, as perfectly phased as synchronized swimmers, and Chris Amado did her own wheelie to bring up the rear. There was something jarringly disconcerting in the juxtaposition of the Mad Dogs' dirty beer-gut bodies and the consummate skill and grace with which every one of them handled a motorcycle. It was like seeing a hippopotamus perform a pirouette.

Rock had been waiting for the call; five minutes after Big Buck had come within a few inches of mashing Chris Amado's brains into the carpet the night before, Apeman and Rock were on the phone together. "Only thing is," Apeman finished up, "we're gonna keep your chickie. She'll ride with us to the meet. That way we don't have to worry so much about you tryin' to pull some kind of kick-ass ambush." Apeman listened for a moment, then burst into his awful laugh as he hung up.

"Rock says we better not let you see our backs," he told Chris, chortling. "Says if you get the chance, you might stomp on us all by yourself. Some kidder, that Rock."

Chris didn't bother to answer. Rock wouldn't let her get in the way of a bushwhack; he'd cut her down along with the Mad Dogs, if that was his play. She was pretty sure it wasn't. This parley had to come down if he wanted to avoid war. Her job was to make sure the alliance never jelled, and to set the Outsiders and the Mad Dogs gnawing at each other's throats. That was her primary concern—that and living through the night.

But as it turned out, Apeman must have put out the word, because none of the Mad Dogs tried anything. In fact,

Diablo gave her the VIP tour so she could report back to Rock how big and bad the Dogs were.

The weapons she'd seen on the ground floor were about to be shipped; the main armament supply inventory filled another warehouse floor. Chris saw Army-issue M1911 .45 automatic pistols and M16A's, along with the Ingram M-10 and M-11 machine pistols that were so popular among the ''cocaine cowboys'' of southern California and the Florida coast. There were Israeli Uzis, Italian Beretta assault rifles, even Russian AK-47's, along with silencers, M-79 grenade launchers and cans, and C-4 plastic explosives with blasting caps.

''Check this out, Princess,'' Diablo said proudly, holding out a collapsible fiberglass tube.

Chris did not have to check it out; she recognized the SAM-7 shoulder-launcher. With this heat-seeking missile, one man could bring down a commercial airliner. Outside of the military, the SAM-7 had one application: terrorism. Its presence, along with the other Russian-made armament, suggested that the Dogs' tentacles reached beyond organized crime, all the way to the shadow world of international urban guerrilla terror. It was the richest market for illicit arms; marking up four or five hundred percent, you could make a fortune in one shipment, if you did not mind living with the knowledge that the guns you were selling helped abduct and murder innocent people.

One room on the floor below housed a printing press for forging identification documents. Piled in another were factory cartons containing radios, stereos, and other electronic components. A third room was a communications center nearly as sophisticated as Dennison's Back Room. A rack held a dozen police scanners, labeled with the five boroughs and cities in western Long Island, southern Connecticut, and northern New Jersey. Voice-activated reel-to-reel tape recorders clicked to life and jerked to a stop. Diablo flipped some switches at the control bank and turned up a speaker's gain, and a woman's voice drawled, "Whatchu mean 'pimp'? Ah ain't nevah split nuthin' with no *man*. You need a squealer, you talkin' to the wrong whoor, offisuh." Diablo laughed. "The lieutenant's office, Fourteenth Precinct. We got bugs all over town."

"Don't the cops sweep?"

"Sure. The cops sweep and find the bugs, and they yank them out and our people replace them." The corners of Diablo's grotesque tattooed mask creased with good humor. "We got nearly two hundred cops—patrolmen, mostly—on the monthly payroll. See, Apeman likes to sort of keep track of what the pigs got on their small minds. He don't like surprises."

The clubhouse occupied the second story, and it was like every other clubhouse Chris had seen in the past couple of weeks: a filthy chaos. The furniture was torn broken-down junk; obscene pictures ripped from magazines provided the wall decoration; the floor was sticky with dried beer and wine and whatever else had been spilled there over the course of a hundred balls-out parties. A double-wide cooler full of brew, along with bowls full of reds and yellow jackets and blue heaven, provided the refreshment as the Dogs began to party. Chris had the idea this was a nightly ritual.

A half-dozen sad-eyed hookers had been brought in for the occasion; they worked the string of whorehouses, porno shops, and cheapo electronics stores the Dogs owned up around Times Square. One of them was pinned up against the wall by a biker named Two-Ton, a sumo-wrestler-sized Samoan who wore a grease-stained Hawaiian shirt under his cutoff. He was nuzzling at her neck like a starving man working on a ham bone. The woman stared past him with unfocused eyes, oblivious.

A hawk-nosed, buck-toothed, chinless freak the others called Wiley Coyote sidled up next to Chris and offered her a joint. She took a shallow hit, held it, and exhaled without taking any of the smoke into her lungs. The sweet minty taste meant the marijuana was laced with angel dust, which explained the mindless blank look on Wiley Coyote's ugly features. Angel dust made brain cells blink out like the lights of London during the blitz.

Wiley Coyote rubbed up against her side. "Hey, mama, what say we boogie?" Chris put a fist in the middle of his gut, not very hard. The biker bent at the waist and waddled away. No one else paid any attention. The night drifted endlessly on.

Yet on this morning the Mad Dogs showed no signs of deterioration or hangover; if anything, they seemed charged up. They were ready and hoping for trouble.

Chris meant to see that they got it.

The negotiations over the site of the big meet had involved three calls over the course of an hour, between which the two presidents consulted with their officers. Chris was surprised, and a little troubled, to see Apeman listen patiently to the opinions of Diablo and Big Buck; maybe the guy wasn't as stupid as she'd figured. It would be a mistake to underestimate him—in any way.

They settled finally on a Nebraska state campground south of U.S. Route 20 on the Niobrara River; Rock and Apeman had both been on runs to the place at various times in the sixties, and they agreed it met all the requirements. It was isolated and in neutral territory; the nearest Outsider satellite club was the Manic Mamas in Denver, three hundred miles away. The petty-harassment factor was low; the closest town, Hopewell, was a one-dog burg of a couple of hundred citizens, and the local cops' idea of a crime wave was when some high-school kid brought in a load of fireworks from Pine Ridge, across the state line on the reservation.

The meet would go down in thirty-six hours; both presidents agreed to that. Bikers lived in the present; there was no time like now for seeing to business. Besides, an immediate get-together reduced the chance of either club setting up any cute traps.

By early afternoon the Mad Dogs had been on the road for seven hours straight, except for a couple of quick gas stops. The forced pace was the normal travel mode for the Mad Dogs, Chris realized. She was trying to work the kinks out of her own arms and legs and still maintain control at 100 mph when Diablo dropped back through the pack to ride beside her. "Up front," he hollered into the wind. "He wants to talk to you."

Chris gunned her Harley, threading a line through the double file of bikers and easing into the empty position beside Apeman. He turned and bared his pointed teeth. Dead bugs freckled his hair and beard, but miraculously his suit remained spotless.

"I need me a chick, Princess." He raised his voice only slightly, but its basso cut through the roar of the flock of bikes and the wind's rush. "You wanna help me out?"

"Why not?" Chris yelled, and the slipstream whipped the words back at her.

"We gotta pay our respects to some dudes in Toledo," Apeman explained. "Nigger club, call themselves the Black Bandits. They fucked up, and we gotta show 'em the error of their ways." His rumbling deadly laugh cut the air.

"There's an indie club in Chi-town, the Assassins," Apeman explained. "They got a hard-on for some of the action, so the cocksuckers signed up the Black Bandits—only the Bandits are supposed to be with the Dogs. Then when another one of our satellites, the Banshees outta Akron, won't go over the same way, the Assassins send the Bandits in to stomp 'em. Them nigger bastards killed two Banshees and crippled another. The poor fucker ain't never gonna ride a scoot again." He sounded genuinely touched with sympathy.

"So?" Chris hollered.

"So we gotta go see the Bandits, tell 'em bygones is bygones, take 'em back in as a Dog satellite."

"Just like thta?"

"Not exactly." Apeman shot her another curl-lipped smirk. "First we're gonna stomp a few nigger heads."

"What do you want me to do?"

"What comes natural, Princess," Apeman growled.

They left the rest of the club at a Chevron station under the watchful eye of a frowning middle-aged black man and the curious giggling stares of a crowd of black kids in T-shirts and run-down Keds. Across the street was a liquor store with a high bullet-proof glass partition between the clerk and the customer area; Two-Ton and Wiley Coyote were coming out with armloads of beer when Apeman and Chris pulled out onto the garbage-strewn street. They cruised quietly past narrow tenements and dilapidated frame houses. Apeman kept them under the speed limit. On one corner some older kids had opened a hydrant and were playing in the spray; on another, a half-dozen black youths in matching berets and lime-green pegged pants watched them through dark smoldering challenging eyes. Apeman stopped at the red light and ignored them.

The bar was on a side street between an abandoned storefront in which every window was broken and a vacant lot covered with weeds and brick rubble. There was no name over the bar's door, and plywood had been nailed up over the windows. Apeman pulled to the curb and killed his engine. Across the street two plump black women looked at him and put their heads close together and walked briskly on.

"Here we are, Princess." Apeman swung his trousered leg over the saddle. "Your everyday white folk, out for a brew."

The interior of the place was a mild surprise. There were leather cushions on the booth seats, a big-screen TV, a new-looking jukebox with stereo speakers, a couple of video games, and a polished hardwood back bar with a mirror over it. The air conditioning was a pleasant shock after the humid tar-melting heat of the street.

There were a half-dozen customers in the bar, all bikers, all black, all staring with undisguised rancor at the two invaders. Someone said, "What the fuck . . . ?" loud enough for them to hear. The bartender was a willowy black woman in her twenties who would have been pretty except for the razor scar that highlighted three inches of her jawline.

Apeman walked up to her, put his hands on the bar, showed her his filed teeth, and said, "Hello, bitch."

A Black Bandit at the pool table took a shot, and the ball rolled silently across felt and plopped into a corner pocket. The shooter straightened and held the cue by the thin end. After that no one moved.

Chris put her back to the bar and her hands on her hips, near the grip of the COP .357. They were on enemy turf and outnumbered at least three to one, and no matter how tough Apeman was, this was a piss-poor occasion for idle mouthing off.

"Can of beer, bitch," Apeman said. When the black woman set it in front of him, Chris turned and picked it up, popped the top, and took a deep slug. Apeman chortled his approval; that was his idea of a classy move. He took the can and finished it off, then crumpled the empty in his paw and threw it onto the pool table in the middle of the scattered balls. In the corner of her eye, Chris saw the bartender bend and do something under the bar.

"She hit an alarm button," Chris said. She wasn't having any trouble pretending to be on Apeman's side; he was her only chance of getting out of this alive.

"No shit," Apeman said, as if she'd just reported good weather. To the bartender: "Is Mofo around?"

A broad-shouldered black man in cutoff and shades came through a door at the end of the bar. "Right here, motherfucker."

Apeman stood back from the bar and rested his right hand on the butt of his .45. "Ain't you looking fine, nigger bro." Without looking at the bartender, Apeman said, "Gimme another can of this piss, black bitch."

"Give it to him," Mofo said. The bartender did as she was told.

Apeman wrapped his mitt around the unopened can, turned slightly and fired it into the mirror over the back bar. Jagged shards of glass slid down and shattered into slivers.

The bartender moved down out of the line of fire. The pool player clubbed the cue over his shoulder, the rest of the Black Bandits came out of their seats, and Chris reached for the Magnum in her belt and thought: *We are dead*.

Apeman said out of the side of his mouth: "No guns."

"The hell with that," Chris said.

Before she could draw, the front door tore off its hinges and thirty Mad Dogs poured through it.

"Thanks for letting me in on the plan," Chris managed to get out, before the stomping began.

Chris heard glass crush underfoot, and turned in time to see the woman bartender coming around at her face with a straight razor. Chris arm-blocked and clipped the woman on the jaw with the COP. The bartender's eyes turned up in her head and she went down.

Big Buck had his thumb in a Bandit's face. He applied pressure and the dude's eyeball popped from its socket, hanging on his cheek from the optic nerve like an overripe grape. Two-Ton grabbed the nearest black biker by an arm and leg, whirled once in a full circle, and let the guy go. His head hit a leg of the pool table; it made a noise like a watermelon smashed with a sledgehammer.

Another Mad Dog had kicked in the glass of the jukebox and was throwing handfuls of records on the floor and crunching them under his boots. Wiley Coyote was behind the bar, opening all the beer taps and knocking liquor bottles to the floor. Other Mad Dogs were slashing the upholstery in the booths, kicking in the screens of the TV and video games, pouring beer over the pool table, destroying anything they could reach.

Apeman stood off to one side until the only Bandit left standing was Mofo, held spread-eagled against the bar by Wiley Coyote and Big Buck. He tried to twist away. Buck did something to a nerve at the back of his neck, and Mofo winced and held still.

"You're a lucky fucker, Mofo." Apeman stood facing the Black Bandit president. "You're gonna get a second chance, and everyone knows Apeman don't give out many of them. You killed two of my bros, and you been playin' asshole buddy with them Assassin bastards. Ain't you?"

Mofo stared back. He nodded.

Apeman punched him in the face. "Say it." Blood dribbled from the corner of Mofo's mouth.

"Yeah," he mumbled. "What you say."

"Aw right. I'm gonna forget all that shit, bro Mofo, because you are okay, for a nigger. Also because from now on you are gonna deal with the Dogs. Ain't that right?"

"That's right."

Apeman stared thoughtfully into the other biker's dark face for several moments. Finally he shook his head. "Thing is, dude, we can't let it lie. Other bros start talkin' if we do that. So I'm gonna cut you, and you're gonna let me. You ain't gonna do a goddamned thing."

Apeman reached inside his suit coat and took out a bone haft. He slipped a catch, and six inches of spring-loaded switchblade shot out.

Mofo stared at it.

He did not move when Apeman cut him, deliberate as a surgeon, a long thin trail from earlobe to chin bone, black skin parting to show shocking-pink flesh and white bone below. Blood welled and flowed.

At the door, one of the Mad Dogs called, "Here they come, boss."

"Let's go," Apeman ordered. When Buck and Wiley

Coyote let him go. Mofo slumped to his knees and dropped his chin to his chest.

The Mad Dogs charged out, Chris at the rear. From somewhere off to the right came the gathering crescendo of approaching cycles.

Diablo was waiting a half-block in the other direction. A barricade of trash, cardboard boxes, and baled newspapers blocked the street, except for a gap in the middle, wide as one bike. As the bikers came pouring out, Diablo began to dump the contents of a five-gallon gasoline can over the barrier. Mad Dog bikes roared to life.

Chris rose up on her kick starter and came down. Nothing happened.

Two dozen black bikers rounded the corner and bore down on her. Mad Dogs shot off through the gap in the barricade.

Chris kicked down again. Her Harley coughed and died.

"So long, Princess," Diablo called sardonically. He mounted his own bike.

Chris kicked viciously at her starter, and the bike sputtered and came to life. The Black Bandits were at twenty yards and closing. Chris burned rubber toward the barricade.

Diablo lit a book of matches and flung it into a gas-soaked sack of trash. Flames flared and streamed across toward the gap.

Chris ducked her head and flashed through, inches ahead of the roaring fire. Heat seared across her back and singed the tips of her hair.

Behind her, brakes squealed and tires whined. Metal crunched as a Black Bandit bike dumped, and someone howled out pain.

Chris Amado drew a ragged breath and accelerated to catch the tail end of the retreating Mad Dog formation.

Chapter Fifteen

The first item out of the Outsider support van was the road keg, the spare that went on any major run so that brew could flow instantly while permanent supplies were arranged locally. Most of the Outsiders gathered around for cups of the lager as soon as they parked their bikes and the keg was tapped; they'd worked up a righteous thirst riding all that day across arid, shadeless Great Plains prairie.

Crazy George, as road captain, was directing the layout of the camp, his manic rapid cranked-up chatter running only at about 33 rpm instead of the usual 78. Snake, Zippo, and Bear were handing out tent rigs, camp stoves, and the rest of the paraphernalia to the bros, relaying orders in low voices. Pretty Boy and his partner Rat started gathering deadfall branches for the bonfire. Blinker hovered around the fringe of the group, the little accountant out of place as usual among the rest of them.

Rock stood off to one side, sipping black coffee from a thermos-bottle lid-cup. Lizzie had gone off somewhere as soon as they arrived; she'd been sullen and uncommunicative since he'd left her behind at Gigantic Gene's ranch. She hadn't liked the idea of the Princess going along, either. When she started to bitch, Rock had to slap her around some. That shut her up, but it didn't mellow her out much.

In the next twenty-four hours some serious business was going down, and he had no time for her pissin' 'n' moanin'. Rock and his predecessor brothers had invested nealy two decades in the creation of one of the most powerful and lucrative criminal organizations in the world. Millions of dollars, scores of lives, and the rise or fall of the biker nation over the coming years all depended on the delicate negotiations at the heart of this meet. The bitch was only along in the first place so he could keep an eye on her.

The state park was near the northern edge of the arid Nebraska prairie, not far from the rolling hills that buffered the badlands country of South Dakota. Most of the bros had been up that way on the traditional Fourth of July fun run to Sturgis for the races, but the regular route took them north of Denver through Cheyenne. Nebraska was a state for riding through on your way elsewhere.

But Rock remembered this place from some run or another, and now, looking it over, decided it would do. The only way into the park was a mile of rutted gravel road. Some time in the past it had crossed the Niobrara on a wooden truss bridge, but it had been washed out or torn down years earlier; only the two approach ramps and the concrete pillars supporting them were left, separated by a thirty-foot gap over the water. The campsites on either side were now connected by a footbridge only wide enough for single files of bikes or bikers. The camps were shaded by willows thick enough to afford a degree of privacy and security, and included outhouses and a couple of picnic tables which was more luxury than most of the bros were accustomed to on a run. The layout would provide each club with its own turf, and the natural barrier of the river would reduce the chance of mindless spontaneous head-butting.

Blinker came over and said, "Someone's coming in." Rock nodded; he had already heard the car motor approaching. He had posted one of the brothers at the turnoff to discourage stray door-slammers, so he had an idea what was on its way. This was routine.

The black-and-white was a four-year-old Ford that needed new shocks. It jounced to a stop at the edge of the trees, and the leaf springs whined as the sheriff and his two deputies climbed out. In a county this rural, it could have been the entire force.

Rock was an expert in sizing up cops. He made the sheriff as a basically honest dude who had run for the office because it beat farming for a living; he had probably been mildly surprised when he won. Peace and order held such reassuring charm for him that except in the face of blatant violent anarchy and riot, he would cheerfully pretend that all was serene. He wore a brown Stetson over a tentative placating smile, and a hint of a paunch over his Sam Browne belt, from too much time behind a desk instead of a plow. The deputies were pallid junior versions of their boss, strawhaired yokels who could have been fraternal twins. They hung back, gawking openmouthed at the bikers like zoogoers at the gorilla cage.

"What's up, officer?" Rock said. The rest of the Outsiders stopped what they were doing and edged closer. This was an automatic gesture of solidarity; besides, when a cop tried to hassle them, there was always the possibility of an opportunity for random mayhem.

"I got a complaint from some tourists. California folk," the sheriff added apologetically, as if a rueful tolerance of West Coast idiosyncrasies were something they shared. "Fella claims him and his family was run out of here by a bunch of motorcycle outlaws."

Rock shook his head, as if such a thing were beyond his ken, playing out the charade by the cop's rules.

"I'm not making any wild accusations," the sheriff said. "Just investigating, is all."

"We sure didn't run anyone out, officer," Rock said. "When we rode in, couple hours back, there were some other folk here, sure. We told them we'd be around a day or so, and I guess they figured they'd rest easier elsewhere. We didn't make any threats."

"No one claimed you did," the sheriff said quickly. One of the deputies elbowed the other's ribs and jutted his chin toward Bear, who was scratching himself inside his ratty coat. The deputies nodded to each other and grinned, as if one of the gorillas had just performed a particularly cunning stunt.

"Anyone wants to camp here is all right with us," Rock said. "It's a free country."

"Well, that's okay then." The sheriff hitched at his belt. "Mind if I ask what you boys are doing here?"

"Nope." Rock waited long enough to let the cop's discomfort build a little. "We're seeing the sights. Nice county you got here."

The sheriff squinted into Rock's face, trying to see through the opaque sunglasses.

Rock fished a roll of bills from the back pocket of his jeans. He counted off ten one-hundreds and put the rest back. He fanned the currency and let the cop look it over.

"We're plannin' a little partyin' later on," Rock said, "and we'll need some supplies. Half-dozen kegs of draft, about fifty pounds of steak, the fixings." Blinker came up behind him and offered a list to the sheriff, who stared at it like a haruspex examining the entrails of a sacrificial lamb. "You take the money into that market we passed in Hopewell," Rock suggested, offering it. "Give 'em a chance to get everything together. We'll send in the van around suppertime."

The sheriff took the cash. "This is a thousand dollars," he said, as if Rock could not count that high. "The stuff on the list ain't gonna cost that much."

"The Outsiders always pay their way, Sheriff. You work it out."

"Say, Sheriff—" one of the deputies started.

"Shut up, Herb." The sheriff was staring at Rock. "I'll see that you boys get what you need."

"Much obliged, Sheriff." Rock watched with vague amusement as the cop trudged back to the patrol car, herding the deputies like contrary heifers. The patrol car swerved around and bounced up the road.

There was a campsite near the riverbank, at one end of

the open campground where it commanded a good view of both sides of the river. They put the wall tent up there. Eight people could fit comfortably inside, and it was high enough to allow them to stand. Inside was a double-size folding table holding four ashtrays, four chairs, a cooler stocked with beer, wine, and ice, and a Coleman stove on which fresh coffee was simmering. A pile of something in the corner was covered over with a canvas tarp. Rock refilled the thermos cup and took one of the chairs. Snake slouched in the opposite one, and Blinker took a third, while Bear stationed himself near the door flap. Afternoon sun filtered through the canvas roof.

"We are going to come on cool," Rock said, "and we're going to stay cool. That's the first thing." He was looking at Snake. "You get the word out."

"I don't like it," Snake said.

"All right," Rock said mildly. "But just the same, we play it the way *I* say. The Dogs will be coming in late tomorrow afternoon, I figure. We greet 'em with brew for the crew, crank, reds, anything they want. We treat 'em like bros. Around sunset we fill 'em up with steak and spuds and the works. We show class right down the line, and they'll have to do the same or they'll have shit on their faces. We use psychology."

"We oughta use tire irons," Snake said.

"After chow we get down to business, which is working out some way to get along, at least for the time being. We all know the stakes."

"I ran a computer model before we left, Snake," Blinker said in a placating tone. "In the best case of only a limited war, we stand to lose a little less than four million in the first six months, primarily in the meth franchises and from contract work for the Mafia." He cleared his throat. "Another big expense will be death benefits."

Rock let the last sentence hang in the air. "You see where we're at," he said finally.

"Look," Snake said, "I'm with you, boss. I won't be starting any trouble—but there's always a good chance the Mad Dogs will."

"Of course." Rock went to the corner and whipped back the tarp.

Underneath were six open crates of M16's and Ingrams, along with a box of L-shaped speedloaders and several thousand rounds of ammo. Rock let them get a good look, then covered over the weaponry.

"First, foremost, and always, we are bikers, bros," Rock said in his hard dead voice. "If the Mad Dogs want war, the Outsiders will give it to them."

Chapter Sixteen

It was after midnight when Apeman raised his hand to signal a halt. The sign was repeated down the twin columns. Headlights raked over a blue "Rest Area Ahead" sign, and a half-mile later Apeman swerved into the off-ramp and led them across the parking apron to the concrete blockhouse rest rooms. They were somewhere west of Des Moines.

Chris Amado was bone-weary and her muscles were cramped and spasming. Most of the Dogs, though, were bright-eyed and twitchy and ready for action—courtesy of the generous doses of feelgood they'd been snorting and swallowing at every gas stop along the way. But Chris could not afford to join them, at least not until it became absolutely necessary. The speed high would get her going, sure—but the crash-and-burn could bring her down in a hell of a hurry.

"Having fun, Princess?" It was Apeman, his pointed teeth winking in the moonlight.

"Nothing like a good run to get your head right."

"You ain't pissed off about what happened in Toledo, are you?" Apeman said it as if he hoped she were.

"I like a good joke as much as the next bro." Chris smiled. "Hope you do too."

"What's that supposed to mean?"

"Not much—except it could be that Rock likes a joke too. You and your bros riding in like this . . . a dude just never knows what kind of joke Rock might have in mind." The more suspicion both sides brought to the upcoming meet, the easier her job would be.

"I thought you was one of them, Princess. Thought you was on their side."

"I'm on *my* side, bro. I watch my own ass. I'm just giving you some friendly advice to do the same."

"Why would you do that?" Apeman said shrewdly.

"Look, bro, take it or leave it. Right now I'm after some shut-eye." She turned her back on him, hoping she hadn't overplayed it. She was too tired to worry about it now. The night was warm and humid. She left her sleeping bag strapped to the sissy bar and dragged herself around to the lawn behind the rest rooms. She was asleep seconds after her head hit the grass.

A rough hand on the shoulder woke her up after what seemed like a few minutes, but when she sat up she saw the first red streaks of dawn on the flat eastern Iowa horizon. There was a cornfield behind the rest area, the ears just beginning to tassle. The temperature was already in the high seventies. Around the parked bikes, a couple of the Mad Dogs were drinking breakfast beers.

The only other sign of life in the rest area was a bronze Buick sedan with a fake-leather-grained vinyl top, this year's model, parked at the other end. A U-Haul topper-box was clamped to the rain gutters, and a half-dozen pieces of Samsonite luggage were strapped atop it with bungee cords. A middle-aged woman and her adolescent daughter came out of the far side of the concrete blockhouse. The woman wore an angora sweater and Bermuda shorts, the girl a leotard top and satin gym shorts. They hustled toward the Buick, careful not to look at the bikers, and when they got into the backseat they locked the doors.

A minute later a small boy, no older than eight or nine, came out of the other rest room, hitching at the waistband of his rolled-cuff jeans. He stopped, rubbed at sleepy eyes with both fists, then stared across at the crowd of motorcycles and riders. He started in their direction. The woman rolled down the window of the Buick and called, "Sean! You come back here!" The kid ignored her.

Apeman was guzzling down a beer. Chris wondered if he'd slept at all; his suit was unwrinkled and clean as always. He belched, then crushed the can and threw it on the grass. The little boy stared up at him.

"Mister?" he said tentatively.

"What is it, son?" Apeman rumbled, not unpleasantly.

Chris felt her stomach muscles tighten.

The kid pointed at the Colt strapped over the suit coat. "Is that a real gun?"

"Sure is."

"Can . . . can I touch it?"

Apeman bent, hands on knees. "You bet," he said, paternal as a department-store Santa.

The boy reached out a trembling forefinger and edged it toward the gun butt, eyes wide. He ran the finger down the curve of the grips, then pulled his hand back as if they were red-hot.

A stocky balding man in a neatly pressed green polyester jumpsuit came out of the men's room and stopped in his tracks. Apeman shot a look in his direction. "Was that fun?" he inquired of the child.

The kid nodded several times. "You bet, mister!"

Apeman gave the kid a sloppy pointy-toothed smirk. "Then fuck off, you little pants-pissing cocksucker."

The kid's face turned pearl-white. His mouth dropped open and his eyes exploded with tears. He turned and stumbled toward the man in the green jumpsuit, falling into his arms. The man carried the kid to the Buick and deposited him in the front seat. He said something to his wife in the back and she shook her head in an emphatic no. The man raised his voice and slammed the door on his wife's whimpering.

He turned toward the gang of watching bikers and squared himself resolutely, as if he were about to dive into icy water. *Dammit*, Chris Amado thought. *Just stay the hell where you are, mister.*

The man in the green jumpsuit strode up to Apeman, threw back his shoulders, and put his hands on his hips. The top of his head came up to Apeman's chin.

"You degenerate scum," the man said. "What makes you think you have the right to terrorize my son like that? What did that boy do to you?" He was trembling with fury and fear as he stared up into Apeman's awful face.

"Fuck off, Pops," Two-Ton muttered. Someone laughed.

"Trash," the man spat. "Filthy gutter trash."

Two-Ton pushed to the front of the circle. "In 'bout two seconds, man, you're gonna be garbage."

Chris Amado moved around toward the man. He was a damned fool, and surely not worth jeopardizing the mission— but goddammit, she could not stand by and see him ripped into pieces.

But then Apeman put out a restraining hand in Two-Ton's direction. "Hey, hey, bro," he rumbled. "Be cool. Mellow yourself."

He smiled down at the man in the jumpsuit, who had paled with sudden tardy realization, like a drunk awakening the next morning in a strange bed with three sailors. He gasped at the sight and stink of Apeman's pointed teeth.

"Listen, man," Apeman said to the guy, "sorry about what happened. We were just funnin'. Maybe it got a little out of hand, but no harm done, right? You got my apology, man.''

The tourist looked at him narrowly, as if Apeman had just offered to sell him a wristwatch. ''That's better,'' he said. No one contradicted him, and he seemed to regain confidence from that. ''Someone has to have the guts to stand up to your kind. You people are a disgrace to everything American and decent. You should be ashamed.''

''We are.'' Apeman looked genuinely crestfallen. ''I'm real sorry, man.''

''You certainly are,'' the man in the jumpsuit said, and turned on his heel. A moment later the Buick pulled out and headed west.

None of it made any sense to Chris. As they got ready to ride, she heard snickers and smirking low wisecracks from the other Dogs, and figured for a moment they were ridiculing Apeman's humiliation. But that didn't make sense either.

She only had to wait five minutes for the answer, because that was how long it took the convoy of bikers to catch up with the Buick.

From the tail of the two-column pack Chris had a wide-angle overview of what happened next. No order was given beyond Apeman's all-purpose raised fist, but everyone knew what to do. The Mad Dogs were a disciplined bunch of bastards.

The man in the jumpsuit flashed a panicked white-faced glance over his shoulder and tromped down on the gas, but it was no contest. The overloaded cager redlined at 90 mph, and instantly it was surrounded by bikers as it shot down the Interstate's straight line. Apeman pulled in next to the front fender, Diablo opposite, Big Buck and Two-Ton and Wiley Coyote taking up open close positions inches away from the racing four-wheeler, swarming like bees in an apiary. The car swerved and every bike moved in prescient tandem, precise as a jet-fighter squadron, every Mad Dog superbly mated to his machine, totally in control.

Apeman reached under his suit coat and pulled his chain-drive belt out like a sword. He took a double turn around his fist, twirled it once over his head like a lariat, and slammed it into the car's left headlight. Glass blew away into the slipstream and scattered across the road, and effortlessly the bikers behind him corrected to steer around the shards.

The rest of them had their belts out now. Deliberately, methodically, at 90 mph, the Mad Dogs proceeded to trash the Buick.

A chain whirled in the early-morning sunlight and the windshield's safety glass starred and turned the color of milk. Nearly simultaneously every other window exploded into a similar spiderweb of cracks. Red and amber plastic lenses smashed into pieces, followed immediately by the bulbs below. A chain slammed into the rear and the trunk sprang open. Another chain cut a deep gouge in a fender. Metal smashed metal in a steady hellish chorus.

With perfect balance and utter nonchalance, Diablo leaned out on his speeding chopper, Buck knife extended, and slashed two of the bungee cords holding the luggage atop the U-Haul topper. Suitcases burst as they hit the pavement, spewing T-shirts and bathing suits and suntan lotion and sneakers everywhere. Bikers cut among them like slalom skiers. A tattoo of chains rained down on the U-Haul box until it ruptured, spilling Coleman stoves, Frisbees, fishing poles, and sleeping bags. Goosedown tufted through the air like snow flurries. A little battery-powered TV rolled out and the picture tube exploded; Chris had a flash of its empty eyeless socket staring up at her as she tore past.

With the same communicationless coordination with which they attacked, as if they shared some sort of pack-animal instinct, the Mad Dogs drew back. Apeman drifted his bike to the rear end of the car, let the four-wheeler gain on him.

When the car had a ten-yard lead, Apeman drew his hog-leg .45 and shot out both rear tires.

The tail of the four-wheeler thumped down and sparks

flew as wheel rims scraped pavement. The car swerved slightly and began to slow. Apeman waited until it was limping along at twenty or so before shooting out the front tires.

The Buick coasted onto the grassy median and wheezed to a stop. Strips of vinyl top hung loose, like flayed flesh. The U-Haul topper was split in two like a broken egg. The Buick's body metal was cratered with hundreds of chain-link-size pocks; no square inch of glass was intact.

Apeman wheeled his bike up to the driver's side window. He leaned over and put his fist through the shattered glass. The window disintegrated.

Apeman leaned in through the broken window. The man in the jumpsuit recoiled, his face drawn with horror.

"Have a nice day," Apeman said, and barked his demented laugh.

Chris could see they were all right, at least physically. The insane nightmare intrusion into their everyday vacation reality would likely live with them for a lifetime.

Apeman was watching her for signs of reaction. "Like it?" he sneered as she rode up to him.

"You've got class, bro," she said dryly. "But right now we'd better be riding. You know what they say about all fun and no work." She rode on past without waiting for his answer.

Chapter Seventeen

Rock and Apeman exchanged raised-fist salutes, but neither offered his hand. The meeting was as stylized as court protocol. Behind Rock stood Snake and Bear; Apeman was flanked by Diablo and Big Buck. The rest of the club members were arrayed behind their leaders. Chris moved up to the edge of the Outsider semicircle. Everyone took their time looking each other over; a full minute passed, and no one moved or spoke. The sun was very warm in the western sky. It was around five in the afternoon.

"Welcome, bros," Rock said finally, solemn as an Indian chief. "We've got everything ready for you." He nodded at the campsite on the other side of the Niobrara. A tapped keg sat in a bucket of ice at the other end of the footbridge.

"Only thing is," Apeman rumbled, "we got a fucking problem there."

Chris watched with interest. Here was the first of what she hoped would be numerous petty challenges. The mission had to come down on this night; the next few hours were critical. She had a big job to pull off, and her strongest allies were tenseness, mistrust, rancor, and conflict between the two powerful clubs.

"What's that, bro?" Rock said pleasantly. His face was wooden as always, the black holes of his shades like the bores of a large-gauge shotgun.

"Don't see how we can get our van over." Apeman nodded toward the support rig, parked near the footbridge. It had left the New York Mad Dog headquarters the night before the rest of them, meeting up with the bikers at North Platte. Chris had seen them load it, so she knew what Apeman was concerned about. The van was full of beer kegs, wine, dope, and other run necessities inside—but the late-model Chevy rig was also carrying enough automatic weapons for a brush war.

"We'll keep an eye on it."

Apeman pursed his fat lips, then nodded. Still looking at Rock, he grinned and commanded, "Unload 'er, bros."

A half-dozen Mad Dogs saw to the job; everyone else watched, rapt as playgoers—and in a way this *was* theater.

The Mad Dogs unloading the rig made certain that everyone got a good look at the crates, ostentatiously exhibiting each as it came out the back door and was freighted across to the campsite. Everyone knew what they contained.

"Tonight we party hearty," Rock announced when the show was over. "After that, we parley."

"Yeah," Apeman said. "Hope you got something to say that I want to hear."

Mad Dog bikes rumbled back to life and thumped over the wooden planks of the footbridge in single file. When the last chopper passed, the van backed up to block access to anything but foot traffic. The Mad Dogs started to set up camp, fanning out downstream toward the old approaches to the washed-out bridge.

"Looks like you pulled it off, Princess," Rock said. "I got to admit, I thought you were dead meat."

"Thanks, bro," Chris said sweetly. "I think you're aces, too."

Rock let that pass. "Come on. I need to know what went down."

Snake and Blinker were sitting at the table inside the wall tent. Lizzie was there too, standing in a corner and ready with a quick hostile scowl for Chris. Lizzie wore a leather bikini bottom and a T-shirt; her arms were crossed over her big free-swinging breasts.

Rock sipped coffee and watched with his dead-eyed stare while Chris told her story. "The bottom line is this," she finished. "That son of a bitch Apeman is completely unpredictable. There's no way you can trust him, and there's no way you'll ever be able to."

"I still say we bushwhack the fuckers and stomp the shit out of them," Snake muttered.

"They've got a hell of a lot of firepower," Blinker pointed out.

"So do we."

"Rock has a better way."

"I don't think so," Chris put in.

Rock stared at her speculatively, and again she had the queasy feeling that he saw through her like glass. "You got something against an alliance, Princess?"

"No. But I've got plenty against Apeman. You're dealing with a lunatic."

"Yeah," Rock said evenly. "I figured that part out, Princess." Without looking away from her, he added: "Tell them, Blinker. Most of it's your idea."

"It's a sort of organizational system." Blinker was proud of his creation. "An infrastructure that gives both clubs autonomy, but binds them together in a way that strengthens both and provides for orderly cooperation and communication."

"Talk English, Blinker," Snake said.

"Rock is going to propose to Apeman the formation of a national council called the Mother Club. A biker board of directors. It'll consist of Apeman, Rock, and five reps apiece from each club's network of satellites. Everyone contributes to its operating budget. It'll be the Mother Club's job to set policy, settle disputes in a peaceful manner, and direct joint operations. Otherwise, the two clubs keep on as they always have."

"Shit," Snake said. "Next thing, we'll all be wearing suits like that Apeman freak. Maybe get haircuts and shaves too, start drinking white wine instead of brew."

"One more thing, bro," Rock said. "I'm going to sweeten the pot for Apeman. I'm gonna let him be chairman of the Mother Club for the first year."

"He'll be paid a salary of two hundred thousand dollars," Blinker added.

"Nice round figure," Chris said.

"It's what the President of the country gets," Blinker said. "We figure the president of the Mother Club is going to be at least as powerful."

"Well hell," Snake said, "why stop there? Why not

hand him over the whole show? Throw in our scoots, too, just so the fucker knows how much we love him. 'Cause as soon as we get out of sight, Apeman's gonna start grabbing with both hands anyway.''

"Easy, bro,'' Rock said. "Part of the deal is that each club will have a full-time observer with the other club. I think Apeman will buy it. Rock smiled thinly. "I'm going to make him think the price is right.''

Chris lit a cigarette. It could work—and if it did, the bikers would be unstoppable. Fragmented into small satellite groups across the country, but commanding the full strength, intelligence support, and financial and political pull of the Mother Club, the biker nation would be the match for any local law-enforcement agency. It would take federal action to put any kind of dent in operations—and right now they didn't have time to wait for the feds to gear up. That's why she was here.

Dennison had taught her the basic fact of their life: there was one way to fight outlaws, and that was outside the law. If they used a rock or a club, you used a bigger one. When they started a fight, you made it a fight to the death.

And you won.

Rock and Apeman were a complementary study in brains and brawn—which made Rock the more immediately dangerous. Chris guessed that the Outsider president had an ace up his sleeve.

Rock had to know that Snake and the other hotheads among the Outsiders were right: Apeman had no conception of honor. Greed, lust, brutality were Apeman's intimates; loyalty was a stranger.

So Rock would try to maintain the balance of power by playing to his new partner's appetites. He'd co-opt the bastard by making sure he and the Mad Dogs had an extremely profitable first year under his Mother Club leadership. He'd put Apeman in a position where even he could see that open warfare would be costly and inefficient. Rock was visionary enough to take the long view and give concessions now against strength and profit in a few years.

Rock had patience—and anyway, accidents happened among bikers. In a while, after the alliance was solidified and the Mother Club running smoothly, Apeman could run into trouble—like a couple of silenced .22 rounds in his thick gorilla skull. Before his gross body stopped twitching, Rock would have taken over the whole show.

Mouthing around a plan like that at this stage would do nothing but threaten security. But once the alliance was set, the future was inexorable—unless Chris Amado stopped the alliance now and for good.

"Blinker?" Rock said at the table.

"The van got back twenty minutes ago," the mild-mannered biker accountant reported. "The brew should be flowing by now."

"All right." Rock stood. "Now, let's get out there and party hearty, and for Chrissake keep everything cool."

As Chris followed Snake and Blinker out, Rock said in his low soft voice, "Hold up, Princess." He ducked through the tent flap, Lizzie hanging onto his right arm. The physical connection swelled her confidence, and she glared at Chris with withering disdain.

"What do you think, Princess?" Rock said.

"What I said—don't trust Apeman unless you've got him on a damned tight leash." The numbers were running down, and she had to start pushing now. "I think you're planning to come down on him—sooner or later."

Rock nodded, as if there was an idea that required consideration. "Anyway, Princess, you've done real fine," he said after a moment. "So far a bro could not ask more."

"Thanks, bro."

"The only trouble is," Rock said, "Lizzie here thinks you're a snitch."

She did not take her eyes from Rock's blank black-shaded stare. "What do you think?"

"I don't know," Rock said, as if genuinely perplexed. "It could be. I don't think you're a cop—I never heard of a cop getting in as deep as you have. Maybe you're working for Apeman—anyway, I wouldn't want to see you hanging around too close with him or the Dogs tonight."

Chris didn't like that part much. Her first idea had been to plant some suspicions with Apeman, try to get his rusty gears turning with distrust.

Some of the other Outsiders, sensing trouble like a bat senses a stalactite, moved closer to them. Pretty Boy pushed to the front, flanked by the always bewildered-looking Rat.

"Maybe you're some kind of private cop," Rock was saying. "Or even some good-hearted square."

That was the truth, and Chris did not like hearing him say it. "Maybe I'm J. Edgar Hoover's goddamned ghost."

Rock shrugged, as if that too were a possibility.

"On the other hand," Chris pressed, "maybe Lizard Tongue here is on the rag over that little trip to Denver you and I took. Maybe she figures we got it on."

Lizzie's blue eyes flared. "Cunt," she hissed—and then, as if unable to stop herself. "You did, didn't you? You did get it on."

"Yeah," Chris lied. Rock did not contradict her.

Lizzie released Rock's arm and stood with fists clenched.

She was teetering on the edge, but she needed one last push. Any kind of fight or trouble worked in Chris's favor—and might take Rock's mind off his suspicions.

"We had ourselves some partying," Chris sneered. "So why don't you go fuck yourself, bitch?"

Lizzie's body was trembling, her breasts jiggling under the thin material of her T-shirt.

Chris grabbed Rock and slapped a big wet full-tongued kiss on him.

Lizzie howled like a hyena and swung on Chris.

Chris twisted away from Rock and stepped inside the wild roundhouse right, driving her fist into Lizzie's rib cage, not very hard. That was a mistake. Lizzie was a couple inches taller than Chris, and knew how to use her leverage. She got a leg behind Chris's knees, and Chris stumbled over backward.

Lizzie tried to stomp her, and missed by inches as Chris rolled clear. She made her feet and they circled in half-crouches, watching each other with wary malevolence.

All the bikers from both clubs surrounded them now. No one made any attempt to interfere.

Lizzie dropped her right shoulder. Chris went with the fake and caught Lizzie's fist on the arm. It didn't do any damage, but it hurt. Lizzie closed into a clinch and grabbed a double fistful of Chris's hair. Chris found cotton cloth between her fingers and ripped, and Lizzie's T-shirt came off. Someone said, "Aw right!" in a low mean voice, and others laughed.

Lizzie paid no attention. She yanked on Chris's short hair, and involuntary tears obscured Chris's vision. Lizzie pulled her down, smothering her face between her breasts, soft as custard.

Chris gasped and rained a volley of short punches into the bigger woman's bare stomach. Lizzie grunted and released Chris's hair, but as Chris pulled back, desperately trying to regain vision and breath, Lizzie caught her full on the point of her jaw.

Chris's legs went rubbery. She grabbed out again and her fingers found leather. She jerked, and Lizzie's string bikini bottom came off in her hands as Chris went down on one knee. She looked at it stupidly. The tears of pain had cleared, but she was still having trouble focusing her eyes.

Then for a moment she was staring, eye level, at Lizzie's bare ass, before the big woman turned. She held a deadfall branch over her shoulder like a designated hitter.

Chris made her feet and turned half-away as Lizzie

swung. Instead of slamming into the side of her head, the branch caught Chris over the kidneys, and new lights of pain radiated up her back.

The bikers were shouting encouragement and derision.

Somewhere in the back of Chris's pounding head, anger ignited and flared.

Lizzie twisted her big nude body and started to swing again, but Chris caught the branch. Startled, Lizzie stepped off balance and let go. Chris dropped the branch and grabbed the other woman's wrist and went with her weight, using it against her, flipped her off her feet in a flailing arc. Lizzie teetered for a moment on the edge of the riverbank, then slid down the muddy three feet of cutbank into the water.

Chris Amado clambered after her. She was beyond playacting or plotting or anything except blind rage. The bitch had tried to kill her.

Lizzie came up sputtering, and Chris was standing over her, ready. She got both hands around the big woman's throat, squeezing at the same time she pushed her head below the river's swirling surface. Fingernails clawed at Chris's arms, feet kicked at her ankles. Chris squeezed harder. Bubbles popped at the surface and Lizzie's struggles became more feeble.

Strong hands grabbed Chris and jerked her back hard. "Mellow out, Princess," a voice said in her ear. The hands backed her out of the water. Pretty Boy had her left arm, Bear her right. When wet, his ratty fur coat smelled even worse than usual. The roaring in Chris's ears turned into the cheers of the bikers behind her.

Chris felt herself tremble; this time she could not control it. She would have drowned the bitch if they hadn't pulled her off. She knew she would have—and remembered Charley Benjamin, and what five years in the belly of the biker beast had done to him.

This had to be the night she finished up.

Lizzie stood unsteadily, knee-deep in the river, muddy

water streaming down her naked body. She rubbed at her neck and waited while Bear came down to help her up the bank. She did not look at Chris.

"Nice going, Princess," Pretty Boy whispered nastily in her ear. He was still holding her arm. Chris twisted away. She turned and came face-up with Rock, his black gaze boring into her. She could read nothing in the look, and right at this moment she could not stomach any of them, so she pushed past wordlessly and got away from there.

Chapter Eighteen

Diablo sat on the step at the near end of the footbridge, sipping from a can of Coors and glaring out from behind his blue tattooed-on mask. Big Buck came across from the Mad Dog side of the river, stopping long enough to say something in a low voice. Diablo nodded and jutted his chin toward Rock's command tent; Snake was standing out front, talking with Bear. Snake stared back, and Diablo's face opened into a wide challenging grin. Snake took a half-step in the direction of the two Mad Dogs at the bridge, and Bear laid a restraining hand on his arm. Staring back at them, Big Buck straightened and showed a dark grim smile. He hitched at his denim breeches, squared his muscular shoulders, and swaggered off the bridge toward the keg, like the toughest kid in the neighborhood walking onto the schoolyard on the first day of the new term.

Chris Amado watched this pantomime with satisfaction. Tension hung over the camp like smog. Both clubs had orders to stay out of trouble—but to be ready for whatever came

down. It was unnatural and uncomfortable for the rank and
file of the two gangs. They were accustomed to settling
differences with chains and knives and guns, not talk. It was
like trying to train a coyote to herd sheep. The longer the
two clubs were together, the more tense they would become.
All Chris had to do was trip the wire that would uncoil them,
teeth bared and claws extended.

That they had not torn into each other already was
mostly due to Rock's iron-fisted control. Rock's monomania
was impressive and convincing; he ruled the Outsiders because they recognized and were swept along by Rock's
unshakable conviction that he would survive and prevail.
Rock went out of his way to appear different: the dark
glasses, the cup of coffee instead of the can of brew, the
avoidance of most club social occasions. And the other
Outsiders, who had long before accepted the fact that they
were impotent in the world without the mob power of the
club, saw that Rock *was* different: he was a winner, and
they'd better stick by him and do as he said.

So Rock in his own way was as dangerous as Apeman.
He had said nothing to Chris after the fight with Lizzie. He'd
already made himself clear: he had no reason to trust Chris,
and he didn't.

Rock emerged from his tent and said something to Bear
and Snake, who went off in different directions. It was
twilight, a half-hour or so to full dark; at the downstream
edge of the clearing the bonfire was already lit, and the
banquet was almost ready for chow call. Three picnic tables
had been ripped loose of the concrete anchors to which they
were bolted and set in a row to form a biker buffet. Dozens of
bags of chips had been slashed open with Buck knives and
dumped into paper plates; the overflow crunched noisily
underfoot as the bikers milled around. There were plates of
cold cuts and cardboard buckets of fried chicken and potato
salad, along with bowls of reds and yellow jackets and blue
heaven. At one end of the tables several kegs had been

tapped; at the other, Bear was unwrapping white butcher paper from fifty pounds of steaks and arranging the meat on the grill over glowing charcoal.

"What do you think, Princess?" Rock was standing at her side. He watched Bear begin unwrapping the meat. His voice was low and flat.

"I think he wants your ass in a pine box," Chris said. "He wants a showdown, right here. What do you figure those chatterguns are for?"

The crates the Mad Dogs had unloaded from their support van were piled near the end of the footbridge on their side of the river. As they watched, Big Buck crossed over with beer for the Mad Dog assigned to guard the arsenal.

To Chris's distress, the food, brew, and dope seemed to be cooling the two gangs out somewhat. Bear finished slapping the meat on the fire; he rose and scooped a handful of coleslaw from a cardboard bucket, stuffing it in his maw; mayo dribbled from the end of his beard. The Mad Dogs who noticed offered polite grins in response to this show of class. Two-Ton passed a joint to Wiley Coyote, who toked, seemed to consider, and passed it on to Zippo of the Outsiders. Chris grinned sourly into the gathering darkness: they were like children, wanting to make friends but unsure in their grasp of the ways of communication and sociability.

"They want trouble," Chris pressed. "If we don't start it, they will."

Rock stared at the subdued partying bikers and didn't answer. Apeman, holed up somewhere across the river, hadn't put in an appearance yet. There had been no sign of Lizzie since the fight; Chris figured Rock had banished her for starting the rumble.

"I say Snake's right," Chris insisted. "I say Apeman wants a fight here and now."

Rock looked at her for the first time. "I think you're the one who wants a fight, Princess. Why?"

"I told you why," Chris said sharply. "The sooner we put down Apeman, the sooner it's over. We'll have it all, and no one will be strong enough to touch us. If we don't, Apeman is going to jump us, soon as he can, and for sure when we are off-guard, when he knows he can wipe out every Outsider in one quick roundup, easy as pigs in a slaughter-house."

Rock shook his head. "You're a smart chick, Princess. You know that if we rumble here, no one wins and a lot of bros on each side die." Rock stared at her through the black lenses. "That's what you want, isn't it, Princess?"

"You're talking bullshit."

Rock took her arm above the elbow. His grip was iron, and his thumb stabbed painfully into her tricep. "Who are you, bitch?"

Before Chris could answer, someone near the picnic tables howled in pain or outrage. "God damn you, you fucking nigger asshole."

It was Crazy George, scrawny as a pogo stick, hopping on one foot and holding the other away from him as if it were on fire. He hopped toward Big Buck, took a two-footed stance once more, and grabbed a fistful of the front of his cutoff. Big Buck raised a menacing hand, four fingers straight out in karate readiness.

Rock released Chris's arm. Apeman came dogtrotting across the footbridge, Diablo on his heels. He and Rock pushed their ways into the midst of the gathering mass of pushing bikers.

"Crazy George!" Rock snapped.

The rail-thin crank-freak turned uncertainly, as if the name were familiar but he could not quite place it. Chris came up behind Rock. Crazy George's eyes glowed with the reflection of the fire and inner unnatural Dexedrine light. He opened his mouth and closed it again several times, like a trout on a riverbank.

"Bastard," he shouted at Big Buck again, and tried to

charge him. Zippo and Bear held him back. Big Buck crossed his heavily muscled arms over his chest and looked amused. George began to mutter some demented speed-talk liturgy; spittle drooled over his chin.

"George!" Rock repeated sharply. Crazy George raised his head and focused his red-light eyes. "What is this?" Rock demanded.

"Goddamned nigger pissed on my foot," George screamed. "Lookit." There was a thin line of wetness down one of his pants legs, which may or may not have originated in his own bladder.

With a sudden burst of speed-freak strength, George tore loose. Before Zippo and Bear could grab him, George put his fist in the middle of Big Buck's face. After that it didn't matter; here was a fight made, and everyone knew it.

Apeman, his .45 Colt strapped on over his clean suit, reached Big Buck's side. "Play it easy, bro," he muttered to Buck. "Thought I told you to stay out of trouble," he added.

Big Buck shrugged. "Been mindin' my own business. Can't help it if this crazy white boy is eating whites like they was potato chips." A little string of blood leaked from the corner of his mouth.

"All right," Rock said. "It's over now."

"No it ain't," Big Buck said.

For several moments none of them moved. Buck was staring at Crazy George with quiet awful menace. George stopped struggling and frowned, as if trying to cut through the speed cloud in his mind to remember what had brought them to this.

"He hit on me," Buck said.

Everyone knew what he meant: when a bro is attacked, every other bro rallies to stomp the attacker. Chris darted her eyes, mentally reviewing firing lines, escape routes, barricades.

"We ain't rumbling." The speaker, to Chris's surprise and distress, was Apeman.

"No fighting," Apeman repeated. "This is about makin' peace."

"He hit on me," Buck insisted.

"I said no—"

"One on one," Rock cut in.

Someone drew breath sharply. It would be nothing like a fair fight. Big Buck had six inches on Crazy George and outweighed him two to one.

Rock was sacrificing Crazy George for the sake of the alliance.

"Fuck it," Crazy George said into the silence. "Fuck it and fuck you all."

He reached a hand behind him and Zippo slapped his knife into it. George brought it around and flicked the catch, and six inches of razor steel snicked out and glittered in the firelight.

Big Buck took a step back and slipped out of his cutoff. He wore no shirt, and his massive slab of chest shone ebony in the firelight.

Crazy George screamed like a madman and lunged, slashing for Big Buck's throat.

Big Buck eased to one side. He moved with great grace and agility, though he did not seem to hurry. His chop caught George in the neck as he went by. George dropped the knife. Big Buck's kick hit at the base of George's spine and he flopped on his face in the dirt and stopped moving.

Big Buck picked him up, flipped him over, and held him cradled in his arms like a baby. Big Buck crouched, one knee up, the other on the ground. Crazy George opened his eyes and looked desperately into the grinning black face as Buck slammed him down.

Crazy George's spine hit Buck's raised knee. There was a sound like a small-caliber rifle shot.

Buck dropped the broken body and stood. No one spoke or moved, except Apeman and Rock, who were staring at each other as if deep in conversation.

"It was an accident," Rock announced.

"Everyone understand that?" Apeman challenged.

No one answered.

"Zippo, Bear," Rock ordered. "Take the van and get rid of him."

Zippo was staring down at his knife. "No way." He looked up. "He was my bro, Rock. A bro dies, you send him off proper."

"We got no time for proper," Rock said. But other Outsiders were grumbling among themselves. It was dawning on them that Rock had let the bastard nigger Mad Dog kill their bro. They didn't know how much they liked that.

"You do what I say, bro," Rock said in his low menacing voice.

"It's for the best, bros," Apeman said in a curiously conciliatory voice. "Best for everyone."

Jesus, Chris thought with disgust. By every rule of biker behavior, guns should have been out and blazing at the first trouble. Instead Rock and Apeman were acting like two frat brothers practicing the secret handshake.

"All right," Rock said before anyone could argue further. "Break it up and get back to partying." He glanced around, saw Chris nearby. Apeman watched Rock move up beside her. He bared his filed teeth in a hungry grin. Rock nodded pleasantly and waited for Apeman to turn to the beer cooler.

"I liked George, Princess," Rock said, watching the rest of the bikers crowd up to the table as the steaks came off the stoves. "We been riding together almost fifteen years. But he fucked up." Rock shrugged. "You I've known maybe two weeks, and I'm not so sure I like you much at all."

Apeman strolled up on her other side, carrying a can of Coors, smiling paternally in the direction of the partying bros. He nodded his monkey head at Rock, the two club presidents having a courtesy social visit before business, like ambassadors at an embassy cocktail party.

166

"What the hell is this about?" Chris demanded. This looked to be drifting toward trouble.

"Ain't no love between me and Rock here," Apeman said out of the corner of his mouth, still watching the others. "We'd just as soon kick ass as look at each other. But that don't have anything to do with you bad-mouthing him and the Outsiders to me, back at that rest stop in Iowa."

Chris looked at Rock. His expression didn't change, but he knew. "I was fucking with him," Chris said, "trying to put the bastard off balance. It didn't mean anything."

"What I figure," Apeman went on, "we can't trust any two-faced bitches." He looked at Rock. "Not any of us. Right, bro?"

Rock looked at her. Chris felt pinned between their gazes. "I don't care who you are, Princess. Hell, for all I know, you could be playing straight. I don't give a fuck."

"We ain't gonna be twisted around by some troublemaking cunt," Apeman insisted.

"The fact is, Princess," Rock said, "I got no use for you anymore—and I can't take any chances."

"I'm a bro, goddammit," Chris snapped in a low fierce voice.

Someone grabbed her from behind. A hand clapped over her mouth, another grabbed her wrist and twisted it up behind her nearly to the shoulder blade. Pain flashed through her arm socket. She looked back, and found her face inches from the grinning clean-cut features of Pretty Boy.

"Princess," Rock said, "you ain't shit."

Chris stared into the dark pools of his eyes.

"Get rid of her," Rock said.

"Fuckin' right," Apeman growled.

Pretty Boy walked her around the side of the tent. His little boyfriend Rat grabbed her other arm, his acned face split in a sadistic grin.

"You remember what I told you, Princess—nobody turns down Pretty Boy." The blond biker twisted harder on her arm, and she grunted with pain. "Now I got a chance to prove it."

Chapter Nineteen

"I like it," Apeman rumbled. "President Apeman—got a ring to it, ain't it, Diablo?"

"There's details—"

"We'll work 'em out." Apeman wiped his mouth with the sleeve of his jacket as if the offer of power had triggered a Pavlovian response. "Numero Uno." He grinned. "The big enchilada." He finished off the beer in front of him, crumpled the can, and tossed it against the canvas wall of the tent.

At the other end of the long table, Rock watched impassively, a vague humorless grin curling his lips. From the first sign of trouble, nearly a year ago when his intelligence sources reported the ascendancy of Apeman, Rock had refused to dismiss the Mad Dog president as stupid. Sure, the son of a bitch had the reputation of being as mean a badass mother as any bro in biker history, and from what Rock heard about him, first in the identity of Creepshow Crenshaw, then as Mad Dog chief Apeman, it was a reputation honestly earned. Even so, some of the guy was flash: the clean uncreased business suit, the matted fur covering most of his head, the jack-o'-lantern pointed teeth. Rock could see through that shit; hell, everyone had his own act.

Rock nodded pleasantly at the rival biker. No, Apeman wasn't stupid—but Rock sure as hell was smarter.

Rock cupped his hands around his ubiquitous cup of coffee. A lantern in the table's center threw drifting light on the walls. On its other side, Apeman in his suit and filthy tangled hair and beard was a grotesque parody of some corporate board chairman.

Whatever turned the fucker on, Rock thought. He knew Apeman would go for it; like most bikers, Apeman lived for whatever he could get his hands on, here and now. It was old scooter-tramp habit: when your life revolved around fast bikes and faster violence, you did not give a lot of thought to the future.

"I'm in charge, right?" Apeman said across the table, eager as a schoolboy appointed hall monitor.

Rock turned both hands palm up, like a stage magician miming nothing up his sleeve. "Day to day, you run the show, you make the decisions. At board meetings of the Mother Club, majority rules. You got veto power, just like the President of the U.S."—Blinker had been right: Apeman had gotten a big kick out of the idea of the identical salary—"but a two-thirds vote overrules you. Of course," Rock added disarmingly, "half the board will be from your clubs."

Rock had no trouble sounding sincere. He wasn't bullshitting the guy; everything he said was true. Oh, sure, maybe he was leaving out a few details . . .

For the next year, Rock did not plan to interfere with Apeman's administration, not directly. Behind the scenes was another story. The Mother Club would give Rock and other top Outsiders direct, aboveboard access to presidents of the Mad Dog satellites—while the Outsider observer would actually be infiltrating the Dogs themselves. Then, as the new structure established itself, Apeman would begin to make mistakes.

Rock would see to that.

At first there would be minor security leaks, nothing serious. Then bikers would be arrested, on the testimony of informers. Both major clubs would be affected; Rock did not mind sacrificing a few Outsiders. Revenues would start to fall off, drug couriers would be ambushed, the cops would seem to know more and more about operations. The word would get out: *Apeman ain't doing so goddamned good, is he, bro?*

By then, no one would be too upset if some unknown party put a long-range rifle bullet through Apeman's monkey skull.

Apeman gazed at Rock with an expression that was as close to goodwill and camaraderie as his ugly face could fashion. The dumb-shit bastard. Once he was gone, there'd be no need for the Mother Club. Outsiders—Rock himself, actually—would run the show, and the other clubs would fall in line behind him, or be stomped. Rock figured on a two-year timetable that started with this meeting. By then he fully expected to be the sole head of the most powerful criminal organization in the world.

Apeman turned in his chair. Diablo and Big Buck flanked him like courtiers. At the other end of the table, Snake and Blinker backed Rock.

Diablo's tattoo mask creased with his frown. "I see problems."

"Then we'll solve them," Apeman growled.

"That's right," Rock said smoothly. "We can hammer out the major details now, and take care of anything else that we think of over the network, during the next week or so. The important thing now is that we've got ourselves a deal that will work."

"I hope so," Snake snorted.

"Not to worry, bro," Rock said easily.

Apeman began to list a few of the minor items that had to be decided, but in a minute he had lost interest and was chortling instead about his plans, the power and wealth he'd be enjoying. Rock pretended to listen, absently nodding his encouragement, but there were other things on his mind. For starters, Snake had to go. He was doing too much bitchin'; that had to be nipped before it spread to any of the other bros. There wasn't room in this club for someone with his kind of ambition, Rock decided. Besides, Snake had outlived his usefulness. He'd just have to be taken care of, like the Princess. . . .

Sure, there was a chance she had been what she claimed. Hell, without her this meet might not have happened. But why take chances—and anyway, Rock had never much approved of women as bros. Chicks were chicks, ginch was ginch. And there was plenty of ginch to go around anytime you felt the urge.

Pretty Boy had permission to do her up any way he wanted before he and Rat offed her. Pretty Boy wouldn't forget the favor, and it cost Rock nothing. Hell, maybe the Princess would enjoy it. A lot of these chicks who liked to act tough would beg for it, once you got them in the mood.

"I need you, Pretty Boy," Chris Amado moaned. "Don't make me wait for it anymore, please."

The narrow single-bed-size mattress in the back of the Outsiders' support van was standard biker issue: it was covered with filth and smelled like a sanitary landfill. Chris lay on her back, her arms tied behind her and her ankles bound. Pretty Boy's clean-cut face eclipsed the dome light in the panel truck's cargo bay. His features were contorted with hate and vengeance. She had humiliated him; she had turned him down. He knew how to handle chicks that pulled that shit.

He crouched next to the mattress and held the straight razor's blade over her right eye. "You want me, don't you, bitch?"

"I've got to have you," Chris murmured.

"Make me believe it."

"Do me, Pretty Boy. Do me once before you kill me."

His eyes brightened, and the razor blade disappeared from Chris's line of sight: the juxtaposition of sex, violence, and death had turned the sick bastard on. Looking past him, she saw Rat, thin and gawky as an adolescent girl. His skin was shiny in the light, and his eyes glowed too, with the anticipation of seeing a woman hurt. Probably one had hurt him, years before; after that he made sure it would never happen again, by sticking with men.

They had walked her around the camp through the trees, keeping out of sight of the partying clubs; Rock didn't want any Mad Dog to get the idea there was division within his ranks. Pretty Boy kept his hand over her mouth and her arm jammed up within an inch of breaking. For insurance, Rat covered her with a nickel-plated .38 automatic, the gun twitching in his delicate fist.

They came out of the woods a half-mile up the road leading out of the campground. They waited for ten minutes; Pretty Boy passed the time tying her, gagging her with his dirty neckerchief, and describing in a low toneless monologue what he was going to do with her. Mostly it had to do with blades, gun barrels, and the sadistic sexual fantasies of a vicious and disturbed mind.

Her execution was not a snap decision on Rock's part. He had given orders to Zippo and Bear before they left to dispose of Crazy George's broken body, because they pulled the van to a stop without any signal. Bear helped them dump her in the back before he and Zippo walked back toward the party. Bear's fur coat smelled like three-day-old road-kill.

The trip took about fifteen minutes. Rat drove, while Pretty Boy rode in the back next to where she lay, playing with his razor and Rat's .38 while he continued his monologue. He wished Rock hadn't ordered him to kill her, he said. He liked the idea of her living a long time—with no tits or eyes or nose, and a face carved up so ugly that people would vomit looking at her.

There was no sound of other cars or anything else after Rat turned off the ignition. Chris saw bright stars through the windshield and the windows in the rear double doors. Rat sidled between the front seats and Pretty Boy returned the pistol to him, then crouched and told her to start begging for it. If she begged for it, he'd give it to her, and maybe not even cut her. Only she better make it good, or he'd cut her anyway. She could die quick and well fucked, or slow and painful.

"I've got to have you, Pretty Boy," Chris said again. The ropes around her wrists were too tight, and her arms were starting to go numb.

"You're gonna have me, Princess. You're gonna be hanged like you never been banged before. You're gonna think a stick of dynamite is going off between your legs."

His face moved away and Chris felt the razor part the ropes holding her ankles together. Her leg muscles tingled as blood rushed into them.

Pretty Boy set the open razor on the floor and roughly pushed up her legs, then knelt between her knees. He leaned forward and reached for the button of her leather pants.

Chris drove her right knee up between his legs, felt his manhood crush as the impact rammed the organs up into his scrotum. Pretty Boy's blue eyes went wide and then closed as he passed out from the pain. Chris tried to roll away from his bulk and halfway made it, had to lever one leg from under his deadweight.

Rat fired the .38 and a slug punched through the van's side wall, six inches from Chris's head. She made her feet, hands still strapped behind her. Rat blinked and tried to fire again. The gun clicked as a bullet jammed, halfway from the magazine to the breech. Rat stared down at the gun incredulously.

Chris twirled in a full circle on her right foot, extending her left. The side of her heavy boot slammed into Rat's temple hard enough to send a jolt of pain up Chris's leg. With her hands tied she could not keep balance as she followed through with all her weight, and she went down, her knee slamming into the small of Pretty Boy's back. He did not move.

Blood was trickling out of Rat's left ear, but his thin chest rattled with his breaths. Pretty Boy was still. Chris sat up and scuttled on her butt to the open straight razor. It took a few minutes, but she managed to cut the ropes without slitting her wrists.

She used Rat's automatic on the lock of the stand-up cabinet in the van, mentally crossing her fingers. One door bent and sprang open. The emergency arsenal was still there: two Ingram machine pistols with speedloader magazines and two suppressors, the HK M300 .22 Magnum rifle for long-range work, a Remington M1100 Magnum twelve-gauge semiautomatic shotgun with the barrels cut to eighteen inches, a foil-wrapped brick of C-4, fuses and caps, some disposable plastic-strap cuffs, and assorted handguns.

It would do. It would have to.

Pretty Boy lay facedown on the mattress. Blood was oozing out from under him. Chris wrestled him over. The front of his pants was soaked with red. He had no pulse.

Rat was easy to move, light as a child. As Chris cinched the plastic cuff to his wrist, his eyes fluttered and opened. "Two of everything," he muttered in a weak voice. "I'm seeing two of everything."

Chris prodded him painfully with the .38's silencer. "I want Pretty Boy out of this van. I can't do it alone."

"You're gonna leave me tied to. ." Rat's high voice trailed off. "You can't do—"

Chris laid the gun barrel along his jawline, not very hard. "You do not say another word." Rat's mouth clamped shut.

She left them in the narrow pit, Rat curled up and moaning and staring stupidly at the bloody mess of dead flesh lying beside him. The van was parked on a narrow dirt tractor road between two endless fields. Chris jockeyed it around, hearing the swish and snap of cornstalks as she bulldozed through them. There were more important things to worry about. Two hundred yards ahead, the dirt road cut a two-lane blacktop, identified by a sign with a silhouette of Nebraska and "Rte. 97" on it. She had ridden in on this road less than eight hours earlier. It seemed like weeks. She turned right and spewed gravel as she gunned the van back toward the camp.

Chapter Twenty

"First off," Apeman said, "what are the Outsiders pulling down monthly from the crank trade?"

Rock's eyes widened behind the opaque shades. The deal did not include free Mad Dog access to Outsider operations. Blinker bent over Rock's shoulder and started to say something in a low voice. Big Buck pointed a finger at him and snapped, "Speak up so we can all hear, little bro." Blinker's mouth clamped shut like a sprung trap, and he straightened quickly, careful not to look at the big black Mad Dog glowering at him.

"Hey, bro, I ain't pulling no muscle-in play," Apeman said openly. "Fact is, I'm willing to give you our territory. You handle manufacturing for the whole country—that'll cut down costs—and we'll provide protection and payoffs, whatever you need. You distribute to us in big lots, we distribute on the wholesale level. You and me, we'll mark it up ten percent cross-country—hell, they've got to buy from us—and the Dogs'll take the markup as our cut."

"What the hell?" Snake rumbled.

Rock stared the length of the table. Suddenly Apeman had turned into someone else, and Rock did not like this new cocksucker one goddamned bit. The gross simian strong-arm man who held onto his presidency by stomping anyone who bitched was suddenly talking like some kind of J. Paul Fucking Getty.

"And?"

"And what?"

"What do you want, Apeman?"

Apeman shrugged and showed his awful grin. "You're selling guns out of Hawthorne, right, south of L.A.? Nice going, bro—but you haven't done much to develop your market. All you got for customers are them dope people coming up from Mexico and S.A."

So the son of a bitch had a man in the Death Lovers, the Outsider satellite in charge of the weapons franchise. There was another idea Rock did not like.

"You ain't thinking big, bro," Apeman went on. "But the Dogs, hell, we could make some money down there."

"How's that, bro?"

Apeman put his elbows on the table. "Let's say your crank business is bringing in about a quarter mil a month." He got up, went to the cooler, and fished out a Coors.

Rock shot a look at Blinker. The figure was accurate. The Dogs not only had a man planted in one of the satellites—they had access to the Outsiders' goddamned master financial records!

Apeman sat down. "On the other hand, running guns to dopeheads is bringing in less than a hundred grand. So . . ." Apeman spread his hands. "I'll trade you the crank for the guns."

"The fuck you will," Rock exploded, and regretted the outburst immediately.

"Be reasonable, bro. This way, we all make money. See, we got connections, far as guns are concerned. We been dealing in Europe with some of them terrorists. They're assholes, but they got bread. They'll pay eleven, twelve hundred for a Uzi and a couple of hundred rounds; hell, they'll ante up four hundred for a used M16. Fuckin' foreigners." Apeman shook his head. "Anyway, turns out there's plenty other terrorist gangs, all over."

"Imagine that," Blinker murmured sarcastically.

"Sure," Apeman went on. "Central America, S.A., all over the fuckin' Pacific. With the Dogs takin' care of business, we're gonna go big-time. We'll be all over the fucking map."

I'd like to be all over your fucking map, motherfucker,
Rock thought. But before he could respond, Two-Ton and
Bear pushed through the tent flap. As sergeants-at-arms of the
two clubs, they were the unofficial peacekeepers and observers.

"What is it?" Rock said, more sharply than he'd meant.

"Everything's cool, bro," Two-Ton said.

"Except," Bear cut in, "for that half-assed Dog dude
who's trying to get one of the Outsiders to knock the fuckin'
chip off his shoulder."

"Who?" Apeman said, not looking around.

"Aw, hell, boss," Two-Ton said. "It's just Scruff."

Apeman grinned. "That Scruff." He shook his head like
an indulgent parent. "Thinks he can take on a whole 'nother
club all by himself." He looked solemnly at Rock. "Once I
saw him do it."

"Aw right," Rock said impatiently. "Get it cooled,
Bear—and for Chrissake, no trouble."

Rock waited until the two hulking bikers went out. The
interruption had given him a chance to digest this bullshit.
Just what the fuck did Apeman think he was trying to pull?
Maybe the bastard was drunk. "Look, Apeman, I thought
you understood this Mother Club idea." Rock smiled and
kept his tone reasonable, pleasant, two bros passing the time
of day. "It's all worked out. We're agreeing not to step on
each other's territory, but we're not teaming up."

Apeman drained the can of beer and crushed the can in
his ham-sized fist. "That's what you think, bro."

Chris Amado had the glob of C-4 plastic explosive in
place and the time-delay detonator "bug" embedded in it
when the Mad Dog guard tripped over her leg. So far, luck
had run with her; she only had to wait ten minutes and two
beers before the guy with the M16 who was watching the
Dogs' Harley hogs wandered off into the darkness. She
listened to his stream splashing on the leaves as she molded

the charge to the underbelly of the Sportster gas tank on a chopped hog at the end of the line of parked bikes.

She became aware that the sound had stopped only as she finished—and a moment later the guy's black leather boot hooked her ankle.

The biker went down on one knee and let go of the M16's barrel to catch his balance. His face, three feet from hers, reflected surprise—and he tried to bring the autorifle around.

Chris sank the Ingram's suppressor in his bare gut and triggered the little gun. It coughed discreetly and the guy fell away from her.

She crawled back to the bike and set the bug on a twelve-minute delay, then wrestled the bulk of the dead guy the few feet to the river's cutbank and lowered him to the water. He sank under its surface without a bubble. Chris followed him in up to her chest, holding the Ingram above the surface as she silently crossed, ten feet downstream from the footbridge and the bonfire's flames.

She came up on the opposite bank where the Mad Dog panel van, parked at the end of the footbridge, was between her and the partying bikers. She molded another charge to the side of the rig's oil pan, set the bug for ten minutes, then wriggled out soundlessly and slipped back into the trees.

"We can play this smooth, bro—or we can play it rough as a washboard gravel road." Apeman was not smiling.

Blinker sucked in air through his mouth. It was too stuffy inside the wall tent; he was suddenly aware of the ripe smell of the other bikers.

"Think it over, Rock," Apeman said generously. "Take your time. Take two, three minutes if you need to."

Big Buck pulled a can of beer from the cooler and set it on the table in front of Apeman, then returned to stand over the cooler. At the same time, Diablo eased over so he was

178

blocking the tent flap. Blinker looked from one to the other through his thick-lensed glasses.

Rock's mind was racing. Apeman was trying to take over the show—and not by following some grand two-year plan, either. The bastard was ready to fight it out here and now, winner take all, if he didn't get what he wanted.

Apeman popped the top of the fresh beer and guzzled it down. Suds soaked into his dirty beard.

Rock made a show of scratching at his chin with his left hand—to draw attention from his right, easing under the lip of the conference table. A little .32 automatic, a belly gun, was duct-taped to the underside, the slide charged, a little gut-reamer slug in the breech. There was the most satisfying solution: pull the gun free and put a slug in Apeman's balls—but goddammit, starting a war was still a losing proposition. Anyway, gunplay inside the tent was chancy—a little bad luck and he was dead. Rock liked that possibility least of all.

The alternative was to give in—or pretend to. Of course. Rock smiled to himself. Say yes to the son of a bitch; hell, suck up to him if you have to. That gave time for planning— that was the key, that was Rock's strength and Apeman's weakness: scheming, working things out, covering the possibilities. Let the guy make you look like an asshole for now—then see how you look in a couple of months, when his brains are leaking out of a third eye in the middle of his goddamned gorilla forehead.

Blinker edged toward the tent flap. Diablo showed him an unpleasant grin and did not step aside.

Without looking at Blinker, Apeman said to Rock, "Sending your boy for reinforcements, bro?"

Rock showed both hands, palms out. "I told you before, bro. We aren't here to start a war."

"That's good, bro, real good." Apeman finished the beer and cocked his head in Diablo's direction. The tattooed biker stepped aside. As Blinker went out, he heard Apeman say, "Aw right, Rock—start making some offers I can't refuse."

Blinker paused outside the tent. Two-Ton and Bear had apparently cooled whatever trouble had flared. About ten yards down the riverbank in the clearing, the bikers from the two clubs were milling around the tables, sloshing down plastic cups of beer, grabbing up pieces of steak with their hands, talking in subdued voices. This was still no balls-out fun run; tension remained part of the atmosphere. But at least so far they'd all kept the reins on their natural desire to bust heads and kick ass.

Blinker went around to the other side of the tent and undid the front of his pants. He stretched his neck back and drew in a deep breath of fresh air. He lowered his head and was absently watching his water splatter on the dirt when he felt the gun barrel in the small of his back. No one spoke. Urine dribbled over his fingers. He did up his pants and wiped his hands on them and raised them to shoulder height, then turned around, moving slowly and carefully.

"One thing you ought to know first," the little accountant said. His voice was surprisingly calm and steady. "It wasn't Lizzie who fingered you. Rock didn't give a shit what she thought. She was a jealous bitch and he knew it, and he would have ditched her pretty quick anyway."

Blinker pushed his glasses up on his nose. "I was the one who got Rock thinking about you. I spent plenty of time in the righteous world. If I learned one thing working for the legal crooks, it was how to smell a phony. You've got that kind of stink all over you."

"Turn around, Blinker." Chris Amado gestured with the suppressor of the Ingram.

The little biker surprised her. "Maybe I have to take it—but I don't have to take it in the back."

"Goddammit, turn around."

Blinker drew a deep breath and opened his mouth to holler.

Chris clamped a hand over it and jammed his head back. It bounced off the low branch of a cottonwood. Blinker clawed for her face. She laid the Ingram against his temple. He bit at her palm. Chris hit him again in the same place, and Blinker went limp and slid down the length of the tree trunk.

She used up precious seconds grabbing him under the arms and dragging him into the riverbank brush. The little biker was an embezzler, whoremaster, drug pusher, and several other varieties of felon, but he was the only one of them who was not addicted to mindless bullying violence. He was scum, but he was not a murderer, and Chris Amado was not his executioner. She was giving him a gambler's chance to live through this night.

Standing against the tent wall in its shadow, she could hear Rock's placating tone. He was saying something about how peaceful coexistence was the important thing. The details would take care of themselves. There was plenty to go around.

Inside the tent a can of beer hissed open. For a time there was silence. Chris checked the LED readout of her watch. She had three minutes before the charges went off and hell broke loose in the encampment. The partying bikers who weren't blown away could take care of each other, but she'd have to take care of Apeman and Rock herself before she could call the mission accomplished.

She was starting to wonder if she had cut the timing too closely—when Snake stuck his head out of the tent flap and hollered for Zippo. Zippo separated himself from the bonfire crew and went inside.

"Find Blinker." Rock's voice carried through the tent's canvas.

"He ain't with the rest of us," Zippo said.

"I didn't ask where he ain't."

"Go with him, Buck," Apeman said.

Chris set her back against the tent wall and brought up

the Ingram, setting the selector to full automatic fire. The charges would blow in ninety seconds.

"Maybe your bro ran out." Big Buck's voice came from the front of the tent.

"If you gotta tag along, keep quiet." Chris heard the snick of a pistol's charging slide jacking a slug into the chamber.

"You watch your mouth, bro," Buck rumbled as they came around the side of the large tent.

Chris stepped out of the shadow and whispered, "Hands up and freeze."

Zippo had the automatic. As he tried to level it on her, Chris stitched a silenced four-slug burst across his chest.

Big Buck exploded with an ear-piercing karate scream and launched his coil-spring body into the air.

Chris held down the trigger of the Ingram and fired wildly, spinning out of the way. The edge of Big Buck's stiffened palm chopped at her neck, missed and grazed off her shoulder, but still hard enough to cause an explosion of pain in her upper left arm. Chris stumbled back as Big Buck hit the ground with a dull limp thud. Her finger was still squeezing the trigger. She shook her head, released it, and reversed the speedloader magazine, jamming the full end up into the receiver.

Except for the eerie echo of Big Buck's scream and the soft crackle of the fire, the camp was silent.

Chris edged forward so she could see the bonfire. Everyone seemed frozen. Bear and Two-Ton, the sergeants-at-arms, were holding guns on each other and the rest of the bikers.

Across the river, the first charge blew.

Fire and smoke and noise blossomed out of the last Mad Dog bike in the row, and then the secondaries went off like a string of huge firecrackers, each gas tank blowing to spew burning fuel over its neighbor, like some rudimentary demonstration of the concept of the chain reaction.

Two-Ton said, ''Goddamned double-crossing two-faced son of a bitch,'' and shot Bear three times in the chest. Outsiders swarmed toward him.

Before they could reach him, the van blew.

For a moment there was only a muffled thud and a little ball of flame that looked like it was trying to crawl out from under the engine. Then there was a hellish roaring explosion. The van bucked up on its rear wheels like a frightened horse, and red-hot chunks of cast-iron engine block spewed in every direction. As Bear fell away, clutching at his chest, Two-Ton half-turned—and a piston rod speared into the middle of his gut and halfway out his back, like a lance. Two-Ton grabbed it with both hands; the hot metal was greased with his blood.

Flame raced the length of the van, the fuel line acting as a fuse. A heartbeat later, twenty gallons of high-octane gasoline became liquid fire, spewing over the crowd of bikers like napalm. Human torches screamed and staggered grotesquely into each other. One stumbled over the bank, and Chris heard the hiss as he hit the river.

From somewhere at the other end of the bridge came rifle fire from a couple of Dogs who had been away from the partying. Someone on this side shot back. From her quick count of the bikers near enough to be hit by the explosion, Chris figured three or four from each club were alive and unhurt.

They'd have to take care of each other for now. Chris had more important business.

Thirty seconds had passed since Big Buck's dying scream had signaled the beginning of the holocaust. There was no sound from inside the wall tent, no moving silhouettes cast by the lantern light.

''Come on in, Princess.''

Chris spun around and leveled the Ingram on the tent flap, bracing the folding stock into her elbow. Rock's voice was maniacally calm.

Chris waited. Behind her the screams diminished as men died. Bursts of sporadic autofire sounded from both riverbanks.

The tent flap eased back. Rock stood just inside it, staring at her from behind the veil of his shades. Using his thumb and one finger, he eased the big Colt revolver out of its low-slung holster and tossed it underhanded outside, then raised his hands.

Chris pushed him back with the suppressor end of the Ingram and followed him inside.

Diablo was lying on his back beside the table. There was a dark hole in the middle of his face where the bridge of his nose had been, and dark red-black blood was smeared over the blue of his tattooed mask. Apeman was on the floor at the near end of the long table, at Chris's feet. He was curled up in a fetal ball with his back to her. He did not move, and she caught a glimpse of blood where his hands clutched at his middle.

Rock sat down at the other end and smiled at her faintly. "You got lucky. When you sprayed Buck, a stray slug took out Diablo there." He gestured at the corpse. "That caught Apeman's attention. We had a little quick-draw showdown, just like in the cowboy movies. I won."

Apeman's big .45 lay on the dirt behind him. Chris stooped quickly and scooped it up, stuck the barrel in the waist of her leather pants.

"Mind if I put my hands down?" Rock said conversationally, and did so without waiting for an answer. "Take a seat, Princess," he offered.

Chris moved around Apeman's body and stood at the end of the table, the Ingram leveled on Rock.

"What've you got in mind now, Princess? You gonna shoot me down, finish up the job?"

That made the most sense—but she could not do it, not in cold blood, not while he stared at her through those dark holes.

"Blinker was right, wasn't he, bitch?" Rock's voice

went icy and toneless. "You're a double-crossing cunt, aren't you? Finish it off, cunt."

Chris did not move.

Rock barked out a laugh. "Having trouble, cunt? Figured you might. Okay, then, I got no hard feelings." Rock scratched at his chin with his left hand. His right hand dropped casually off the edge of the tabletop. "You done me a favor, killing off the competition and all. I'm gonna be king-shit of this operation after all." Rock straightened a little in the chair. "Soon as I take care of business."

Chris heard the tearing sound and squeezed the Ingram's trigger without thought. Twin slugs thudded softly into Rock's chest and he catapulted over backward in the chair.

Chris came around the table. The .32 automatic lay a few inches from Rock's outstretched hand, the strip of duct tape that had held it under the table still stuck over the barrel. Blood bubbled from Rock's mouth and pulsed from the two holes in his chest. His dark glasses had fallen off, and in the lantern light he stared up at Chris through eyes that were the palest blue, almost unpigmented. The light made him squint. He said, "Cunt," almost dispassionately, and closed his eyes. He made a choking rattling sound somewhere in his throat and did not move.

Chris let out a long ragged breath. Outside, the gunfire went on. She backed away from Rock's body and turned for the tent flap.

A hand vise-gripped her ankle.

Blood covered the middle of the front of Apeman's elegant suit. His little pig eyes glowed with elemental pain and fury.

Chris tried to bring the Ingram around, and he yanked with incredible strength. She went down half on top of him, her face inches from his. His breath was rotten and decayed; he smelled like spoiled meat, and she gagged.

Apeman twisted his head, groping to reach her throat with his deadly sharpened teeth.

185

Chris felt the heat of his noxious breath on her skin. She pulled with desperate strength, got the muzzle of the Ingram around, and clamped down on the trigger.

Apeman's huge body bucked and arced under her, and one last fetid rank breath burst out of his mouth like an exploding puffball. Chris scrambled away on all fours and stayed like that, trying to catch her breath.

She touched at her neck. There was a dot of blood on the tip of her finger, like a pinprick. She looked at Apeman's gaping mouth: the point of one of his front teeth was crimson, as if it had been delicately dipped in nail enamel.

Chris scrambled to her feet. She dropped the empty Ingram and unholstered the little COP .357, then edged through the tent flap.

No one was shooting. The van at the near end of the footbridge was a twisted, smoking mass of broken, torn body metal; the nostril-flaring stink of smoldering rubber and up-holstery drifted toward Chris. Across the river a Mad Dog behind the cover of the mess of torn-up Harleys began squeezing off single rifle shots at some target upriver. Some-one fired back.

The campground was littered with dead bikers. Two blackened corpses were draped over the railing of the footbridge; another two lay on its deck. They looked like tasteless tar-baby caricatures of human figures. Where the picnic tables had been there was a pile of smoking lumber and bodies.

Chris dropped to a low crouch and streaked across the open ground between the tent and the far side of the clearing. Someone picked her up, and slugs puffed dirt at her heels. An Outsider whom the explosion had missed was ducked among the bikes, looking for a target. He swung around and Chris shot him from five feet. He slammed into a chopper and knocked it into another, and bikes went down like dominoes.

Chris's cycle was off to one side, close to the road for quick getaway. She came down hard on the starter and the big

Harley roared to life and leaped forward, dirt rooster-tailing into the air as she goosed the gas.

She swerved onto the narrow gravel access road, and into the glare of headlights about fifty yards ahead. Above the headlights was a rotating red police beacon.

The cruiser lurched to a stop and the sheriff's voice, bullhorn-amplified, shouted, "Hold it right there!"

Chris slewed to a stop.

The higher-pitched voice of one of the deputies whined, "She's got a goddamned gun."

A shotgun exploded from behind the cover of a car door. Chris flinched instinctively, but she was out of range. She was also out of luck. She didn't have time to launch into any detailed explanations with the county law, and she sure as hell could not shoot her way through them.

She wheeled the bike and gunned it back toward camp. A second futile shotgun shot blasted her backtrail.

The near end of the footbridge was blocked by the ruins of the van. The other end was covered by a Mad Dog rifleman.

Then, in the dim starlight, Chris saw the abandoned bridge approach ramps, fifty feet downstream, the thirty-foot gap between them yawning over the sluggish flow of the Niobrara.

Chris swung her bike around. The old road cut a mostly straight path through the trees. She cut onto it forty yards from the near ramp.

Chris cranked the accelerator to the red line. She did not want time to think this over. She kicked into second and the speedometer nudged the sixty mark. An exposed root grabbed at the front tire and Chris wrestled it straight again. She jolted onto the ramp, cranked out a last nudge of speed, and pulled up on the front of the bike as she cleared and went airborne.

She seemed to be suspended over the dark river for a long time. She watched the opposite ramp approach and braced herself. She was coming down short; five miles an hour faster and she would have made it. The thought passed with something like detachment, and she readied to go limp and roll.

The rear wheel of the bike caught the lip of the ramp. The front tire bucked down with a tremendous jolt, bouncing her high off the seat and almost sending her over the handlebars. She held as the bike settled and found traction. It wobbled and she twisted her body and the bars in compensation. Then the bike was steady again, and barreling down the old road. She went two hundred yards farther on before she remembered to ease off on the throttle. Her bike lurched to a stop.

Faintly, like the noonday memory of a midnight dream, gunfire sounded upriver. She listened to it absently. She shuddered once and then was okay, although her hands went on trembling for a few minutes. By the time she got them steadied, the gunfire had stopped. Behind her through the trees she could see the flickering glow of the van's dying fire. Nothing else moved.

In the other direction the old road emerged from the trees, and Chris became aware of the sound of normal traffic somewhere up ahead. She drew a deep breath, fed gas to the bike, and started back toward civilization.

Dennison's Place
The 24th of July

"Two Mad Dogs tried to run the sheriff's roadblock," Dennison said. "They were killed. An Outsider was DOA at the county hospital. Working back from your original head count, two Outsiders and a Mad Dog escaped on foot."

"Too bad," Chris Amado said.

"I'm satisfied," Dennison said. He paused. "How are you, Chris?"

Chris gazed across the sweep of lawn in front of the mountainside compound. It was pleasantly warm, and a breeze stirred the orange windsock. The sky was cloudless, a washed-out blue color that reminded her of Rock's strange eyes just before they closed.

There was always the hangover. You did not go out and kill and come back the same, not ever. You changed a little every time, and it took a while for all of it to filter through your mind and your emotions. It was something you had to face up to, and that was how it should have been. When it did not tear at you at least a little, when the killing became routine as eating or walking, you were out of business, because there was no longer that difference between you and Them.

"Fine," Chris Amado said to Dennison. "I'm fine."

Dennison sat in his porch lounge chair, a brandy and soda near at hand. Miss Paradise was stretched out on a chaise at the foot of the porch steps, a shimmery pale-blue Danskin covering her long lean body like skin, bare tanned legs slightly parted as she shifted to face the sun more directly. Terrycloth bands circled her wrists.

Chris wore brilliant white twill shorts, sandals, and a pale silk shirt with the top two buttons undone. The last week she had found herself changing clothes once or twice a day; she needed to be clean at all times.

"The one called Blinker suffered a mild concussion," Dennison went on. "He was still out when the sheriff's people found him the next morning."

"What about Rat?" Chris asked. "The one I left cuffed to Pretty Boy."

Miss Paradise shot a look at Dennison. For a moment neither of them answered.

"Dead," Dennison said steadily. "Massive brain hemorrhage."

Chris nibbled at her lip. Rat was as bad as any of them, and as guilty—but dammit, she did not like the idea of having killed him accidentally. It happened; the body was a complex device, and there was no such thing as a "nonlethal blow." And yet; he should not have died. His life was pathetic enough. . . .

"Charley Benjamin is back in Washington." Miss Paradise's eyes were closed and she moved only her mouth. "His people think the fight was a spontaneous blowup; he told them he split and broke cover when he decided the rumble was inevitable. There was nothing more he could do, he said."

She sat up and swung her legs to the ground. There was a sheen of sweat in the valley between her high breasts. "Benjamin's agency took Blinker off the sheriff's hands," she went on, "thanks to a call from the boss here. He's been charged with enough to keep him in jail for seventeen lifetimes, mostly involving wire fraud, income-tax evasion, and conspiracy; apparently he wasn't involved in any of the violent stuff. But as chief accountant he knows everything important, so the Agency is bargaining him down in exchange for full details of the operation: names, places, legitimate business fronts, cash flows, assets, numbers of Swiss bank accounts, the works. Charley Benjamin is heading the interrogation team."

"According to my contacts," Dennison said, "the satellite clubs are jumping all over each other. No one knows which side started the fight at the Nebraska camp, so I've arranged to have a few rumors put out—blaming one gang or the other, depending on who is listening. In the last week we have confirmed reports of forty-seven bikers being killed. Most of them were single hits, but twenty-four died in a head-to-head rumble at a bar in Joliet, Illinois."

"We beat them," Chris said softly, staring across the grass.

"It looks that way," Miss Paradise said.

"Until they wake up and stop fighting each other, and come after us again." Chris looked over her shoulder at Dennison. "Until some other Apeman Crenshaw comes along and bullies them back into power. And it will happen—we all know it will."

"Maybe," Miss Paradise said. "But right now the biker gangs are back where they were a decade ago, disorganized, isolated, and paranoid about everyone, including other bikers. They're out of action for a long time."

"And then what?" She had been melancholy for the last few days, as if suffering some sort of postpartum depression.

"Whatever is necessary—as always." Dennison leaned forward in his chair. His voice was firm, even stern. "Look, Chris, we came into this fight with our eyes open. We're out to win rounds and stay ahead on points, but we're not going for a KO, because we can't realistically expect one. No one wins this fight—but we aren't planning on losing, either. For sure not to scum like Rock and Apeman and the rest of those sick bastards."

"No one knows," Chris murmured despondently. "Even Charley Benjamin's people don't realize what you did. Not to mention the rest of them, the ones in the street who would have ignored the bikers until the boot stomped into their faces. The ones who think it's easiest to do nothing—until it's too late, and nothing is all there is left."

"We're not looking for thanks," Dennison snapped. "We're looking for results." His voice softened. "You know the truth, Chris, and so do we. That's enough."

"It'll have to be," Miss Paradise said.

"Okay," Chris said.

"Get some R and R. Take a vacation."

"Take two aspirin and call me in the morning," Miss Paradise said.

Chris Amado laughed. "All right. I can take it. I'm a tough guy." She stood up and brushed at the seat of her shorts. "Who do you want me to dismember next, Mr. Dennison?"

He grinned up at her, and she bent and gave him a quick tight hug. "Thanks," she murmured, "for letting me help."

Dennison watched her go around the building toward the rear entrance to the living quarters. Miss Paradise came up the three steps to the porch and stood over him. Dennison sipped at the brandy highball. The blue Danskin looked sensually smooth as satin, and Dennison thought he could feel the sun's heat radiating from her bare thighs. Miss Paradise offered her hand. He took it and she pulled him out of the lounge chair.

"There," she said. "You got some thanks after all." Her lips were three inches from his.

Dennison smiled. "I told you: I'm only interested in results."

Miss Paradise rested her cheek against his. "Come along, boss dear," she murmured. Her warm breath caressed his earlobe. "I've got some results you really ought to see."

The Next Adventure
KING OF THE MOUNTAIN
by Adam Lassiter

"You have a long day ahead of you, Mister Vice-President."

With those chilling words, a deadly threat to national security explodes. A renegade CIA-sanctioned former operative has unleashed a brutal paramilitary attack on a secret high-level meeting against which the Secret Service is powerless. Horn's hostage: the Vice-President. His demands: two million dollars in gold, the release of a prized Russian operative—and Dennison as the delivery man. For Horn it is a vengeful lashing-back at Dennison who helped convict him of espionage after he brutally betrayed his troops in the Vietnamese jungles. For Dennison it is a chance to crush once one and for all a festering menace. The improbable war zone: Glacier National Park, Montana —an eerie, frigid wilderness like no other place on earth, in a remote chalet that is a lung-crushing walk in summer and a virtually impassable sheer frozen rock climb in winter. With the backing of a hand-picked cold-weather commando team led by William Sterling Price, Colonel, Special Services, Dennison has only seven and a half hours to complete his suicide mission. Horn has chosen the game and the field, and he may think he controls the rules. But now it's open season in Dennison's War where Dennison lives by only one rule: victory.

The #1 national bestseller—now in paperback!

LEON URIS

AUTHOR OF EXODUS AND TRINITY

THE

H
A
J

Leon Uris returns to the land of EXODUS in a mighty epic of Arab and Jew, hate and love, vengeance and forgiveness to bring to life a spellbinding epic that probes to the heart of a centuries-old conflict . . . a powerful and moving testament that tells one of the greatest stories of our time.

Don't miss THE HAJ, now on sale wherever Bantam Books are sold. Or use the handy coupon below for ordering:

SPECIAL
MONEY SAVING
OFFER

Now you can have an up-to-date listing of Bantam's hundreds of titles plus take advantage of our unique and exciting bonus book offer. A special offer which gives you the opportunity to purchase a Bantam book for only 50¢. Here's how!

By ordering any five books at the regular price per order, you can also choose any other single book listed (up to a $4.95 value) for just 50¢. Some restrictions do apply, but for further details why not send for Bantam's listing of titles today!

Just send us your name and address plus 50¢ to defray the postage and handling costs.

RELAX!
SIT DOWN
and Catch Up On Your Reading!

☐	24707	THE WINDCHIME LEGACY by A. W. Mykel	$3.95
☐	24680	THE SALAMANDRA GLASS by A. W. Mykel	$3.95
☐	24537	THE OBSESSION by David Shobin	$3.95
☐	24607	LINES AND SHADOWS by Joseph Wambaugh	$4.50
☐	23845	THE DELTA STAR by Joseph Wambaugh	$3.95
☐	20822	GLITTER DOME by Joseph Wambaugh	$3.95
☐	22750	THE KINGMAKERS by Arelo Sederberg	$3.95
☐	24493	DENNISON'S WAR by Adam Lassiter	$3.50
☐	24172	NATHANIEL by John Saul	$3.95
☐	23336	GOD PROJECT by John Saul	$3.95
☐	24234	MAY DAY IN MAGADAN by Anthony Olcott	$3.50
☐	23792	THE COP WHO WOULDN'T QUIT by Rick Nelson	$3.95
☐	22753	THE GUNS OF HEAVEN by Pete Hamill	$2.95
☐	25226	OMEGA DECEPTION by Charles Robertson	$3.95
☐	24646	THE LITTLE DRUMMER GIRL by John Le Carré	$4.50
☐	23577	THE SEEDING by David Shobin	$2.95
☐	23678	WOLFSBANE by Craig Thomas	$3.95
☐	23420	THE CIRCLE by Steve Shagan	$3.95
☐	22746	RED DRAGON by Thomas Harris	$3.95
☐	23838	SEA LEOPARD by Craig Thomas	$3.95
☐	20353	MURDER AT THE RED OCTOBER by Anthony Olcott	$2.95
☐	25006	GOLD COAST by Elmore Leonard	$2.95
☐	24606	THE SWITCH by Elmore Leonard	$2.95